GO ON

A queer writer of odd things, **Tania Hershman** lives in Manchester and is the author of three short story collections, two poetry collections, two poetry pamphlets and a hybrid book of poetry/prose/fiction/non-fiction, and what if we were all allowed to disappear (Guillemot Press, 2020). Tania's second poetry collection, Still Life With Octopus, was published in July 2022 by Nine Arches Press. Co-author of Writing Short Stories: A Writers and Artists Companion (Bloomsbury, 2014), she is co-founder of the On This Day She Twitter account and co author of On This Day She: Putting Women Back Into History One Day At A Time (John Blake, 2021). Tania has a PhD in creative writing inspired by particle physics. Go On is her first novel.
www.taniahershman.com

Also by Tania Hershman

Short story collections

The White Road and Other Stories	Salt Publishing, 2008
My Mother Was An Upright Piano: Fictions	Tangent Books, 2012
Some Of Us Glow More Than Others	Unthank Books, 2017

Poetry

Nothing Here Is Wild, Everything is Open	Southword, 2016
Terms and Conditions	Nine Arches Press, 2017
How High Did She Fly?	Live Canon, 2019
Still Life With Octopus	Nine Arches Press, 2022

Hybrid

and what if we were all allowed to disappear	Guillemot Press, 2020

As co-author

Writing Short Stories: A Writers and Artists Companion,
with Courttia Newland — Bloomsbury Books, 2014

On This Day She,
with Jo Bell and Ailsa Holland — John Blake Books, 2021

GO ON

Tania Hershman

ISBN: 978-1-915079-93-0

Cover designed by Aaron Kent and Joe Kent

Edited by Cathleen Allyn Conway

Typeset by Cathleen Allyn Conway

Broken Sleep Books Ltd
Rhydwen
Talgarreg
Ceredigion
SA44 4HB

Broken Sleep Books Ltd
Fair View
St Georges Road
Cornwall
PL26 7YH

for all the women

Tell your own story, and you will be interesting

– Louise Bourgeois

I want to talk, she says. Can you hear me?

I hear her faintly. I say, speak up, but I'm not sure that gets through. So I send a note, via the Author Intermediary provided when we're having these sorts of difficulties. I ask her:

What would you like to talk about?

I say it kindly. Narrators need firm kindness; otherwise they never open up, otherwise there'd be no story at all. But we must propel. Hence: firm. It would be so easy to let a thread disintegrate. I know how to do this, to coax.

She writes back. Does it matter, she writes, if I am not sure what it is yet?

Oh no, I say, because really it doesn't. Whoever knows at the beginning what it is the beginning of? Just start somewhere, I say, and I believe I hear her sigh. I believe I hear her breathe out and pick up the start of it.

Can you hear me? she says.

Yes, I say, although she is still speaking softly. We'll work on that.

I composed. A song for sitting, a song for standing. But one day I'm not sure at all how to put a note next to another note.

This doesn't seem to be the start, she says to me, and I know that a Narrator's job now is to say:

Go on.

I am alone, she says, and I want to be, although this is…

Yes?

Although this doesn't make for a good story, she says, and now I can hear her laughing. I am supposed to not want to be, she says, and there is something different in her voice. Isn't it unusual, for the heroine – I am the heroine, right? – to want to be alone? Not to be chasing someone?

Well, I say carefully, not wanting to close anything down, there are those sorts of stories.

The romantic sort, she says.

Yes, I say, quite traditional, with the desires and the thwarting of them and so on. I can hear her really laughing now. I like to hear her laugh.

What if, she says in between the giggling, I have other desires, and those get thwarted instead?

It would keep me reading, I say, although being a Narrator

is a full-time job, I don't read a lot. Other stories, you know.

Ah, she says, and I can hear her louder now. Well, I think this might work then.

Go on, I say.

I am alone with my notes, and one day, there are no notes and I am alone, and so I walk.

I walk and walk, wondering to myself what kind of woman I am, this woman who had the notes and now has no notes and is putting one foot in front of another foot, trying to find the thing.

But while I walk, I am enjoying the walking, and I am not missing my notes at all, and this is not

such an interesting story, is it?

She stops. She's not laughing.

Happiness at being alone, I say carefully. There might be something in that.

Tolstoy, she says, something about all happy families being alike. He means: 'boring'.

We know about Tolstoy. As Narrators, he's caused problems. He is severe in his ideas about writing. Russians. I can see that I have to tread carefully.

Yes, I tell her, and I hear her doing something, perhaps making herself a drink. I am hoping it is only tea. I have had those problems, too. But what a challenge, I say, to try and write about the thing they insist is boring, shouldn't be written about. I am proud of myself for this one.

Oh, she says. Yes, that's a very good point.

You know, I say, I think one of the other points they make about writing is to find your voice.

I always wondered about that, she says. Surely my voice is already my voice?

This is my comfort zone, narrative voice. I know where I am here.

Yes, I say, but you don't speak in the same way to friends as you do to, say, a student in a classroom, someone in a shop. You shift and adjust your tone, your register.

True, she says. I am not talking naturally to you, for example. I don't know you. You've been assigned.

I'm here to help, I say, but I am not who you are writing for.

Ah, she says. That's the thing. What if I am writing for myself?

When we meet, the Narrators, or as many of us as can get away, in between projects or when the writers are in The Zone, as they call it, and don't need us, we discuss problems. We never get tired of talking about problems. Starting is the hardest, we tell each other. We are usually only brought in for the new ones, the ones who have never tried this before. Yes, occasionally there is an experienced one who wants to experiment and needs assistance, but much of the time, once they have two or three under their belt, they may not know how the fourth will be, but they are happy to go it alone. They know what starting is, and that they've done it.

The new ones, though, try and duck out at any opportunity. Straightjackets, we say. We've had many thoughts about innovative devices to tie them down. We have calmed each other when all we want to do is shout at our Author. A Narrator who is violent is not ideal. That's not helpful.

Endings, we say, of course. Endings are a bugger, we say, and we laugh. We laugh because there's really nothing we can do here at all. We can't put forward an ending; our guidelines are stricter about this than anything else. We can't even suggest possible avenues towards the ending. We could be struck off. It is immensely delicate.

The middle is the best part, we say to each other, opening another bag of crisps.

There is a woman walking through the cemetery. The dead are watching her. There are many of them in this cemetery; it stretches on and on. The dead sometimes take notice of who is going along the paths, the breathing walkers, and sometimes they are tired and they rest. It takes energy to observe those whose hearts are not still. Look at the way they think; they move their heads on one direction and the other, and the blood, the blood!

This woman is interesting to the dead because she is talking to them.

"Hello," she says to a gravestone, and she reads the name on it aloud. She does this again, and when there is more than one name on the stone, she reads all the names. The dead are puzzled. They are used to the squirrels, the diggers, the weeping loved ones. They have long ago stopped noticing those who come every day, sometimes twice a day, for years and years, sitting by the same plot, talking to the gone one as if the gone one was interested, every day, sometimes twice a day, for years. The gone one was flattered at first, who wouldn't be? But who wouldn't want the still-theres to move on? Who wouldn't want the breathing walkers to go, walk, breathe through their newnesses?

This woman is interesting to the dead because she is saying other things. She is saying things to them about their words.

"Why all the 'beloveds'?" the woman asks them. "And the 'went-to-sleeps', really? Is it like that?"

The dead aren't used to this, not from a complete stranger. They ask each other if anyone knows who she is, and the message is whispered down and along, down and along. It gets to the Muslim section, to the part across the road, and even as far as the Jewish graves. But no one knows.

The dead who are lying with, or above, or below, their beloveds, ask, Why is she alone? And the dead and their beloveds say, Wouldn't it be nice if...she had a husband? The very much more modern dead say, Maybe she wants... a wife? They shake their heads as she wanders past them, reading names, looking at one date and the next. The dead don't understand alone. They will never be alone again and many have forgotten, those of them that knew, the joy of solitude. The ones who date back 150 years are not used to seeing a woman on her own, a woman walking on her own, seeming not to be meeting anyone, not to need anyone, doing what she pleases. The dead men are confused by this. (Many of the dead wives are not confused but envious. Not just of the life she has, but that it is hers.)

When she recites poetry to them, the dead feel warm for the first time for much time, although they don't know time any more. They don't know the poems, either, don't know that she wrote them herself. And that being in the cemetery is, for her, a very strange experience, and speaking her own poems makes her calm. It's not strange because someone is dead, has died, will die. It is strange because she is trying to think her way through to solving it. Nothingness.

The woman feels herself not old but not young. It is this in-between. She is one of those who thinks. She sometimes is so overwhelmed with thinking; so often, in fact, that she looks for kinds of distraction. She watches television – but not too violent, she can't take that any more. She reads, although reading makes her think, so not too much.

Is the woman talking to the dead? There is no one there to ask her what she is doing. She is a walker, a thinker, a writer and reciter of poems. She is not someone who expects... not now in this in-between. She walked through here on the first day of the year and wondered if she would make it to the last. Not because she is ill. Not because she wants not to make it to the last day. Simply a wondering. A knowing that she knows not very much at all.

The dead say to her, You don't want to be here yet. The dead wives want to shake her, tell her, Take everything! The dead wives, some who loved their dead husbands, who loved their children and their children's children's children, are sent spinning by the woman's singleness. For the first time, for all time, even though they have no time, they want it back: the moving, the flowing of, the breathing in. They want it back in her. They want in her. They want.

Is it her story? the other Narrators ask me. Is that her? I've told them what's going on, that we're in Beginnings, not in the Middle yet. I've told them that she's sent me something.

I don't know, I say. The woman in the cemetery, I think that might be her. I'm not sure yet.

My colleagues shake their heads. Tricky, they mumble. Best to not ask questions, let her keep going. Don't stop her now.

You might wonder if they can talk directly to you. Authors, I mean. You probably have questions about this. They can, of course. They don't need us. They simply have to lift themselves onto the page.

It works in many different ways. It might be through a character, who is the "I" of their book, their story, their poem. The "I" may be an amalgam – a word we like. How much of this is him, do you think? we ask each other. Do you think she did that herself – hang-gliding over the Amazon; picking up an older woman in a Belgian cafe? We love to chew this over: where fiction and reality touch. We don't know. There is no solid ground here.

Should you trust in whoever is telling the story? Do we trust what the Author tells us? Does our involvement come with a seal of reliability?

No. I'm sorry. That's not part of our remit. We are interested in story. Truth is for philosophers, and they sit at another table.

I can smell it on her. She wants some. Of my energy. She wants to plug herself into my socket. It isn't sex. This isn't that.

She wants what she doesn't have, without overturning what-is to fall into a might-be, unhooked from ropes sometimes velvet, sometimes iron.

I am the shortcut.

I don't want to be a shortcut. I don't want to be plugged into. And anyway, it wouldn't. Perfume is different on each person, I've never been one of those who wafts. I've worked hard for this, for fuck's sake. It's like those who write to me work-wise and ask how I did it, demand a bullet-pointed-list, ask for all my contacts, so they don't have to. When I suggest and point towards, how many don't say thank you? How many don't reply, giddy with my directions – or disheartened because I won't heave them up to where they think they deserve to be? Why should I share?

I do. But when I want to, how I want to, what I want to.

A shortcut is something that saves time, avoids us getting caught, shears off corners, smooths the lifts and plummets. The shortcuts – those back doubles, as someone's father called them – don't care. The alleyway, those streets. They are not there for you.

Her desires rise hot off her, and on her face a taking and a disappointment. Because I will always be. Her own fizz and shift will never last unless she knows how to spin it. I've worked at this, lady. I am my own cocktail; you cannot drink me. Get yourself a saw, a nail file; I am not your prison visitor. There is nothing in my cake but sweetness.

INT: Living room, night.

A heavy breathing is heard from an unspecified direction.
Enter an **ANIMAL**. It is dark. Nothing is seen.

The animal circles the sofa, which is hundreds of years old. The animal sniffs the right arm, swipes and catches its claw, rips free and leaps onto the table.

On the table is a lamp. The animal switches on the lamp, and sits, cleaning itself.

A second animal enters, stage left.
A third animal enters, stage left.

A faint singing is heard, from an unspecified direction. It is a new version of the oldest song. The animals are still. The sofa does not speak. The lamp is on, is on, is on.

A **WOMAN** *is not here. No men or children are here. The lamp is switched off. The lamp is switched on and three animals sit on the ancient sofa. The animals are staring at you. The song has finished. One animal begins to read from any book you choose.*

Choose a book. Choose an animal. There is no space on the sofa. Here is your armchair. Listen.

There is a priest in Ethiopia who every day climbs a mountain to get to his church, carved into the side of the cliff. Part of his climb is a sheer nine-foot ascent. He climbs this every day.

"So far nobody has fallen, because the Nine Saints have kept them safe. The saints that live in these mountains have delivered them."

Why he doesn't live in the church, live by the church, build another church? What is it that is so important? Is it punishment or bliss? Is it the idea of daily ascension that he loves?

Go up.

Go up.

I think she is making herself a mystery, a puzzle. She has sent me several parts now, such different parts, and she is working towards the fitting, but she has no plan, no map. That is fine. Many of them are feeling their way down tunnels, across unlit space. There are also the Planners, yes; but even they take side roads, find they end up where they weren't expecting to be.

She is getting somewhere. We are getting somewhere. We have voices here.

I don't ask her questions, not while she is sending. I can hear her sometimes, hear the effort, but also something else. She is enjoying this.

Go on.

Put them all together in a room.

No, not yet.

You Blew Me Away (8) *Found scrap metal* **Penny Hardy**

There are scientists who study silence. They measure its weight, the volume of it, its texture. Silences are not alike. The team have developed a taxonomy, tools to calculate the properties of each particular quiet.

The silence of the empty home when that emptiness is wanted
is different from the silence when the occupant is lonely

The silence between two people who have nothing left to say
is different from the silence between companions reading

Silence is light, is heavy, fills and unfills.

The silence inside the head cannot be reproduced outside it.

The scientists have put silence in a lead-lined box, have filtered it through water, bubbled it through gas. Some burned silence, others froze it. Silence was dropped into test tubes, rocked and shaken. Silence was grown in a petri dish using nutrients no one else had tried before.

Silence expands and contracts like breath, like hearts. If you want it, you will know how to find it. If it frightens you, you'll know how to drown it out.

Noise is not the opposite of silence. Noise is another country. There are other teams researching there.

I always wanted, she says, to be a cat.

Go on, I say.

It seemed easier, she says. Other people are so odd. So unpredictable. I can spend all this time making myself, figuring out how I want to be in the world, but the minute you step out of the door...

Into the outside, I say.

Oh dear, she says, I don't want to be awful about the world. I don't want to be mean, ungrateful. But it's hard, isn't it?

When they ask you questions, that's when we need to tread lightly. This job, being a Narrator, can sometimes, as I've said, be close to therapeutic. After all, we're helping a person tell their story, or tell a story – if there is a difference there. Our role is to be midwife to it, I suppose. Which is not the same as making it, is it? We're there, at the birth, we can lend a hand, but the creature's formed by them.

Does that sound cold? You can't get so involved in one birth, because that could affect the next one, do you see?

Cats, I say. I figure this is safe territory.

You know where you are with cats, she says, and there is some sighing. Cats do what they want to do, when they want to do it. You know how a cat, in the middle of playing with something, a ball or a mouse on a string, will sometimes suddenly stop and clean itself!

I don't really... I say, not being familiar with cats. Or dogs. There was a book once, but I am not sure how much of that was accurate.

If they want to stop, they stop, she says, and her voice is fading a little. They don't need to explain to you, or to themselves, why it's time to clean. When they're hungry, they make sure you know it and that you give them what they want. Oh dear.

I know, I say, because some of this does sound familiar. When we are together, the Narrators, it can be difficult. Some of us are louder than the others. Sometimes, I...

This is not my story.

Go on.

SINGLE
adjective

1. Lacking the company of others: alone, companionless, lone, lonely, lonesome, solitary, unaccompanied.
2. Alone in a given category: lone, one, only, particular, separate, singular, sole, solitary, unique. **Idioms:** first and last, one and only.
3. Being or related to a distinct entity: discrete, individual, particular, separate, singular.
4. Not divided among or shared with others: exclusive, sole.
5. Without a spouse: fancy-free, footloose, lone, sole, spouseless, unattached, unmarried, unwed. **Idiom:** footloose and fancy-free. See *marriage*

verb
1. To make a choice from a number of alternatives. Also used with out: choose, cull, elect, opt (for), pick (out), select.

Sentence Examples
A **single** image can end a war.
- Could he then merge two souls together into a **single** body?
- But not a **single** person appeared to be in the room.
- To be intoxicated by a **single** glass of wine! I have experienced this pleasure when I have drunk the liquor of the esoteric doctrines.
- He whipped off his belt and added it to the rest of his belongings, leaving a **single** knife strapped to his thigh.

Also mentioned in

- single-mindedly
- non-single
- single-malt
- single-chain
- single-phasing
- monocentric
- singlism
- singletail

Words near single in the dictionary

- singing voice
- singingly
- singings
- singjay
- single-acting
- single action
- single annulus
- single bed

It is a kindness, when there is another who sees. So often there are no others who see. Looking is not the same as. We often now don't. I am not, now. Here is the window and I am not. I look at the window to check what I am not.

I see the non-lookers on buses, in streets, heads down. They do not see me seeing how they do not look.

When a person is seen, on an ordinary day in an ordinary way by another person who is not extraordinary, who has not been paid to see, to listen… it is extraordinary. It can lift an entire day, this been-seen-ness. The eyes, yes. Lift your eyes to.

What is this need we have to be seen?

When I walk through the world, I do not mind, being a woman on her own, being a woman who may do what she likes with her hands, her arms, her money, to be sometimes unseen. This allows me. I look; I may stare for they will not see me stare. The one-direction seeing does not lift us both, only if they – for one second, for the smallest part of a second – glance. Mutual is what makes it. Less and less now. Heads down, they are; and I am with my head up and turning, left and right, up further, too… look at the clouds!

How far does it – will it – go, the non-looking? Will I soon be the only one on the streets who does? Is it witnessing? Does everything need to be seen to be real? And if I miss? There must always be missing; it is not some fear of mine. But I must confess to a specialness in that I see what no one else. It becomes in me: the way she checks herself in that shop window, how he stands and grins at his device, that smile of being loved by one he loves.

I have questions. My investigations of the days outside – are they about my search? If I see enough, will a jigsaw complete itself? I suspect pieces will be always added and I will keep on… keep fitting together some small sections.

I don't mind. Alone in the world, my hands free, my eyes drawn here and there. This is my happiness.

The dead are delighted to see that the woman is back. She is talking to them.

"Did you know," she says, "that there's an institute for cemetery and crematorium management?" She is holding pieces of paper. The dead are confused because they try not to think about the *whereness* of themselves, or of their lack of selves. Some whisper to each other about the word "crematorium", a rustling goes along rows and down, along and down. Burning, comes a reply, there is burning. The dead shudder at the thought of this, though they are already. Dead.

"Service sensitivity," reads the woman from the paper. "The burial or cremation of a human body, whether the deceased is an adult, infant, child or foetus..."

The dead who were children want to tell her to stop. She, the walking-breathing, shouldn't think of this. Don't be here, the children try to say. But she is still talking.

"... a highly emotional occasion for all those taking part."

"Solace," she tells them.

"Respect," she says.

The dead so really wish they could come up, come out, come round her, not scaring, not oh dear but saying yes yes yes we do it's alright don't you don't you no no worry. Burning, they whisper. Talking, breathing, walking. Move on, they say to the woman with the pieces of paper. Move.

Move.

GUIDANCE SUBJECTS

Please see the links below for guidance and downloads on a range of subjects and issues:

- Baby and Infant Funerals – Policy and Guidance
- Body Parts
- BRAMM: British Register of Accredited Memorial Masons
- Charter for the Bereaved
- Environmental
- Foetal Remains Policy and Baby and Infant Cremation
- Health and Safety
- Holding-over Cremations
- Legislation
- Management of Memorials
- Mercury and Emissions
- Pandemic Planning
- P. I. Questionnaires
- Recycling Floral Tributes
- Recycling of Metals
- Reuse of Graves
- Transfer of Rights
- VAT on Funerals

Am I telling my story, she says, I feel that this is all...

Don't worry, I say, you don't have to know anything yet.

Oh dear, she says. It all feels so short. I don't seem to be able to. I mean, it's not one story, is it? I'm getting worried, I have sometimes had anxiety. Should I worry? Yesterday, I was thinking about hospitals, I mean, aren't they amazing: buildings where people can go, can turn up when something's wrong, and there are doctors who will try and help you. Amazing. I was on the bus and I was looking at the pavements and thinking, Gosh, see what we've achieved! Civilization, I mean, but then I look at the news and I think, Gosh. I think, is all we've achieved just better and more efficient ways to... I mean, apparently, I read a book a while ago that says this is the least violent period in human history. It's hard to take that in. It's hard. We've achieved less violence but much greater attention to it. More panic.

I can hear something in the background; I think it's the television.

Go on, I say.

What's so surprising, I tell the other Narrators when we meet, is the difference between her writing and her self. Her writing is so clear, so fluid, so authoritative.

Well, she is the Author, says someone.

Yes, but when we speak, she can barely finish a sentence, it's hard to believe, I say, that I'm talking to the person who wrote what she is sending me.

Do you think...?

Oh no, I don't suspect anything. It's not like that. I suppose what I'm trying to say is that this is the first time I have seen such a gulf between the Author and the writing.

That can happen, says someone else, taking a crisp. They can be unrecognisable, really, you never would imagine. I mean, take crime writers – so many of them, so sweet and gentle, and look what they do to their characters.

That's true, I hadn't thought of that. I suppose, I say, that this isn't a genre, so I had different expectations. If this had been science fiction, for example, I wouldn't expect her to be... No, that isn't it, it's more about the quality of the writing, the style – not the content. She appears, in person, or at least when we are in direct communication, to be tentative, to have a tendency to worry, to panic even. I don't feel that in her work, not at all.

Isn't that why they write? says one of the Narrators. Because it's on the page that they do feel in control?

We all sit for a while in silence after this.

There is a town in which all the women are angry. Although it is a myth that the Inuit have so many words for snow, the women of this town use many, many words for rage:

ire	choler	bile	fury	wrath
outrage	temper	irascibility	dyspepsia	spleen
annoyance	vexation	exasperation	crossness	irritation
irritability	indignation	pique	displeasure	resentment

They take from other languages, too: colère, courroux, rogne, Zorn, Entrüstung, Groll, ghadab, ca'as, hasira, boosheid, gramschap, rabbia, enfado, gussa, fennu, ikari. And they have their own secret words.

There are others in this town: cats, dogs, men, children, some chickens, a goat. This is not their story.

The girls of the town, before they reach the age of eighteen, have classes in anger. Each year the class is taught by a different woman, because rage, like love, is personal. There is no curriculum; each teacher makes her own.

One year, the teacher asks the girls to draw their anger. You might think that there was a good deal of red and black. You might think many things. The pictures they draw are hung in the classroom, and the teacher asks each girl to pick someone else's drawing to talk about. They sit in a circle, the girls and that year's teacher.

"I love the way it's quiet and then loud," says the girl with the dark hair and the small smile.

"I never thought of it as an animal," says a girl who has only recently come to the town and whose voice no one has heard yet. "I never thought of it much at all."

"It's..." says another. "It's just. But I. I can't tell. I don't."

"Yes," says the teacher. "Yes."

Another year, the girls put on a play, and choose to show it to the women, the children, the men, cats, dogs and chickens.

Sometimes a teacher will take the class on a field trip. Sometimes, during the class, everyone will lie on the floor.

A woman accompanies students as they wade in the shallow part of a rocky beach to their school for the first day of classes in Sitio Kinabuksan, Philippines, on 1 June 2015.
LORGINA MINGUITO/REUTERS

Girls attend a class at their school, which was damaged by a recent Saudi-led air strike, in the Red Sea port city of Hodeidah, Yemen, on 24 October 2017.
ABDULJABBAR ZEYAD/REUTERS

The dead women in the cemetery are listening to this story about the town of angry women. They nod their heads at the part about the classes. Yes, some of them say, we understand this. Where is this town? others ask. The question ripples along the rows of graves, around the angels, past the west chapel and the east. We are angry too, they whisper.

Oh dear, she says. We have not spoken for a while and I had wondered what was happening in the silence. Oh dear, she says again. I showed it to someone, that was a mistake, a mistake. I shouldn't have, should I?

Well, I say carefully, knowing how sensitive an Author can be at this particular stage, at the point we are at where things are starting to happen but we have not yet reached "cruising altitude", as one of my colleagues working with a pilot puts it. If you felt the need, I say, to show it, you must have had a reason.

Oh dear.

Sometimes, I say, a thing can be both good and bad. I hear her sigh.

That's very true, she says. I did want to show someone. And it turned out to be good because she liked it, but not so good in that the existence of a reader, well, I don't know. It...

It threw you?

Yes! Threw me, knocked me off balance, made me wonder whether there was any point at all, which doesn't make sense since the person I showed it to wants to read more, but it also does make sense because no one has ever waited for me to write something, because I've never ever shown something unfinished. Well, a draft yes, but not something without an ending, where I haven't even reached it yet. Some idea of an end yet.

This is different from those times?

So different, she says, and has been so different from the beginning. Maybe this is part of that difference, the showing and the being thrown and the return from that, the recovery from it. Gosh, she says, you are so helpful, this is so helpful, talking to you like this. Is that part of your, I don't know, job description?

I pause. We are not really supposed to discuss these things, what our role is, the technicalities, pull back the curtain, as it were. But we are charged with helping our Authors, smoothing the way, and I don't want to not answer.

I am here for you, I say, to assist in the writing down of your story, to help you tell it the way you want to, and that might entail any number of things.

Sending me a crate of whisky, for example? She laughs, and I breathe and I think, Well, we have moved through this. This might, I will tell my fellow Narrators later, have been a serious sticking point. They will say, Well done, you navigated your way. You navigated her way. You helped.

You really help, she says, as if she has moved ahead in time without me, has heard what will be. This sometimes happens too, I am told. Cause and effect. We have had training on this, but I hadn't encountered a possible instance until now. It is an odd feeling.

It's my pleasure, I say. And it really is. I am midwife, and we are progressing.

Go on.

Today I am a man. You would not know to see me, although today I do have extremely short hair and I am conscious of being stared at. I think I am being stared at for it, the unusual shortness of it. I may not be, of course, but who else can tell me if I am?

It is not in the seeing though. Today I am at my deepest a man, in whatever that means. It is a choice, a decision, a switch. It is not perceived by that group, the ones who stared when I arrived, unsure if this was the house. They, all outward men, stared, watched, as I drove past, drove back, turned around, parked, found the gate, opened the gate, and drove through. What would a man then?

I have been reading that there is nothing conclusive found in brains that make mine 'female' and another's not. If you had two brains on a table, a clean dry table, my brain and my brother's, say, there would be no telling. You could not point and declare: "Woman". If you sliced it, still no joy.

[Where is joy? Another question. Is there a centre for it? Or is joy an accumulation? Or a switch-off of misery, pessimism? Is joy a string of neurons all lit up at once, a pathway you have to search for, but when you find it, walk it often, it lights up and up and up?]

Another book I've read describes "priming" – how women do better on a maths test, say, if you tell them beforehand that this is a test on which women do better. What mad creatures we are! Being better at a thing after we are told that others who are – or may be in some way – like us, tend to be better at the thing. Could we not start off everyone in life, whisper when they are babies, Your kind is better at this, knows how to live better, to be better? Would this not catapult us all in the right direction, no matter the small problem that not everyone can be "better" without some being worse?

So, perhaps in saying "Today I am a man," I am priming myself for something, to do something, to not do something.

It is raining. What would a man do? Now here we run into more trouble. There is not one thing a man would do. There is one thing one man would do, and another thing a second man would do, and so on. Some men might do several things, and some men might do nothing at all. Some men might do what some women might do. Do you see how complicated this is becoming? [Where has the joy gone?]

Let us say this. Today, I am a person. A person with, today, extremely short hair, who drives past, comes back, turns around, finds the gate, drives through. A person who sits here listening to the rain. What might prime me to be a person in the world, without the female/male layering, without the cosmetics of all that business? Yes, there is a question of genitals, but do they have to mean so much, mean everything? Where is the line?

If I am the line, if I draw it here, write 'PERSON' on my forehead – not so that you would know to see me, if you looked – what would it do? I am attempting personhood, moving past my genitals, moving past my woman-priming, sliding away. I attempt. There, the joy is back. There.

On the radio, they are discussing whether, after a person's death, an undertaker might allow the spouse or family the use of a finger to unlock a mobile phone. Is this ethical, asks the DJ. An undertaker phones in. No, he says, absolutely not, I wouldn't allow it. A young man sends a message – he and his wife share passwords, so this wouldn't be a problem. A Scottish woman calls up, irate, utterly opposed to a spouse seeing their dead mate's phone because what if... and the conversation is all about how much might be hidden that should stay hidden, even after death. She is angry. No one has a right... The dead must be respected... She is so angry.

The women of the town get together before the beginning of the school year to discuss the upcoming class. The one who will teach it presents her structure: not for the others to judge, because the women understand, they know and feel how rage is a different beast in each of them, and not only a beast, but also a song, a flight, a sword.

They come together to listen, but also to allow each other to disagree, no need for consensus. They come together for history as well, so that in that room – which may not be the same room as the previous year, but is a room they recreate no matter where the space and no matter that the group may be slightly altered, having lost and gained – is the idea of every class across every year and all the centuries. This has been the case for so long that no one remembers the beginning, although they all remember the memory of it, their own first session, the one where they sat waiting and wondering what they would be made to do. ("Would we fight?" they whispered to their friends. "Will we roar? Will they teach us how to tame it? Will they let us let it out?")

Each year they gather, with food and drink, and it's a gathering all the women of the town make themselves available for, and that the children and the men, the dogs, the cats, the goat, cannot make a case for interfering with. No one says, "Where are they all today," although some men and many of the children will, in their heads, think: "But what about...?" and the end of that thought makes them ashamed because this is what their town is, its specialness and how can they. How dare they. Some men and many of the children find other things to do instead.

There is no written account of it. The appointed teacher has her notes, but no one is taking minutes, in particular not of the first hours where they open up about their own angers, their own furiousnesses. The ones that have simmered for 12 months, or the new flare-ups from a week before, the different qualities of these light and heavy rages. There might be shouting, whispers, tears. Not for therapy, not to cure each other, but to add to the tapestry of it all, more stitches, new colours and texture. Anger is a process, a product, a sound, a cloud, everything and nothing, it comes and goes, can be fed or soothed, held or pushed out into the world.

Stripped *B&W RC print & ink, photo taken by Kyong Park, 1995.* **©Shirin Neshat**

COURTESY OF THE ARTIST AND GLADSTONE GALLERY

Hannah loses herself, I read in a feature article. She apparently forgets who she is – they call it a "fugue" state for want of a tidy fix, an explanation – and she wanders away from that life. I read about the first time, how she disappeared before she was to teach the first day of school. Not that she was new to teaching, she was young but experienced, she enjoyed it, mostly. But they couldn't find her. She stopped sending messages, she wasn't home.

Her mother and her friends start looking, the article says, and after a week or two there are reports. She's seen going into a restaurant but by the time a friend turns up, she's gone. She is slippery. They get closer and closer.

And then a boat. She is found in the water. Alive. Alive, swimming and really with no idea how she got there, no answers to their questions.

Here is their conclusion: They think that for those weeks she wasn't "Hannah".

["fugue" – from (or to) "fugitive"?]

They think something happened and she lost that thing we assume we can never lose: our *self.*

As I read I'm trying to figure it out along with them. The writer of the article is giving me clues, has made choices in what she tells us, as if to suggest something. Is Hannah too kind, too invested in other people and their happiness, not selfish enough? Does this mean her grip on her *self*ness is looser than yours or mine, and something – some slight stress – can let it go? I notice myself thinking as I read,: "Why didn't she take better care of her *self*?" and as I think that, I think: "Why am I blaming her?" and: "Is it so terrible that she, for a few weeks, steps outside her*self?*"

In hospital, she can't explain it to her mother or her friends. Her mother comes to terms with this, which I think says a great deal about her own *self* or grasp, or lightly holding on. (The father, too, somewhere far away, a religious man who always – when she visited – took Hannah travelling, and is sure, when asked by the writer, is absolutely certain, that this constant movement cannot have made her feel unsettled, he him*self* is certainly not the cause). Her mother wants, the writer tells us early on, for the journalist to make it clear that she doesn't see this as a situation to be "fixed", a mystery with a solution that will one day be found. It is what it is. How astonishing for a mother to let her daughter, her slipped-*self*/slipped-off daughter, simply be, to not need to grip her, lock her in a tower, say "for your own safety...."

I started to know, as I read the article and there was no interview with Hannah

["fugue" – as in "fog" or "fug"?]

that she isn't here anymore. We only heard her through the others and isn't that a point we are learning about *self* – ours is made up by us and by our others, the ones who see us closely, who tell us what we've been and how we've been, and expect that we will be that through time? What if Hannah wanted a break? A break-up with her self, which she couldn't do in their faces, could only do if she slid out the back door, leaving behind – as she did that first time and the next time and the next – her phone, her wallet, her keys?

The last time she was seen, she was working as a teacher on an island before an enormous storm. Again she slipped away. She is out there now, or in the now of the end of these few pages. In the writing of her she has been fixed, but fixed – at the insistence of her mother and the agreement of the journalist – in her unfixedness, her sliding *self*hood. She may not be in the world any more, which might mean death or mean the death of "Hannah". Her friends say that wherever she is, whatever *self* she has now, they are sure everyone around loves her because that's who she is.

But it isn't. It's who she was to them. No one can know, even we can't grasp, who we are when we are alone. Are we what we react to? This is the tune that philosophy, psychology, biology are beginning to sing, which Buddhism has been whispering for centuries. We are not solid, fixed through time, not to ourselves and certainly not to anyone else. We are not born with it all, and there is never a moment where – like hair, toenails, skin – we stop, still breathing, knowing we are baked and done and ready.

["fugue" unlike "effigy"? Unlike "configuration"?]

Hannah, when she was twice found, was found in water; water was where "Hannah" came back to her*self*. Is water the most similar to us – a jar-bound liquid, pushing at the sides, wanting the lid screwed tightly on, but also wishing for some small leak, some small heading out to sea.

[blankness]

Here's the thing, she says, and I think that she wants to talk about writing, discuss where the narrative is going, a shape that might be emerging.

It's about sex, she says.

Oh, I say. I am unsure what to say. This really is not my remit.

Sex, she says again. I have never really had any.

I stay quiet. I have no idea how to respond.

The thing is, she says, I haven't had much of it, because, well, no one has wanted to have much of it with me.

Is this...? I say, and wonder whether I should say what I am thinking.

Is this relevant? she says, and she laughs. I am relieved she's laughing. I laugh a little too, but not in a way, I hope, that makes it seem as if I am laughing at her. Relevant, she says. That would be easier to answer if I knew what the hell I was writing about! Although something does seem to be coming through, doesn't it? That last piece, about self and identity, I found it very moving to write. Anger, identity. I mean, sex has something to do with it, no? A person's identity as a sexual being, that's what I never felt. I thought it would come, no pun intended. I thought it was something that a person did, every person, it was a part of being grown-up. I thought.

There is silence and I hear her blow her nose.

This is hard for you to talk about, I say.

Yes, she says.

You don't have to.

It's good, talking to you, she says. I feel like you want to help me, that you aren't judging me, you want to let me let it out, so I can find...

I do, I say.

Find my story, she says.

Yes.

This is making it better, she says. I won't ask you, don't worry, about you or anything. I don't even know if someone like you... Well, anyway, that's not your job, and you're not my therapist either. But this might need to be in there, in the story. Or maybe it is already in there and the anger is something to do with. I mean, frustration. Frustration and ideas about being, about personness, about how to project yourself in the world. About how I am to others, and how I am to me. You see, to me I am a sexual person. And should it matter at all if it's something private? Should I be bothered, upset, that it's rarely involved anyone else? Well, yes, because I am – we are – surrounded by it, by people having it, wanting it, doing it, with other people. But not me. Okay, yes, it's not only me who isn't. I imagine millions of people around the world aren't having sex either, have never had sex, or don't want sex, or want it but no one wants to have it with me. I mean, them. Look at the slip of my fingers there!

I don't believe it's only you, I say. From what I have read, there are entire books, entire libraries written on the subject of what goes on between two people. It appears very fraught.

Yes! she says, and I am glad to have said the right thing. Oh yes, oh dear, so fraught. And who says if you are doing it, that it makes life so much. Better, I think I mean. Better. What if it simply makes life...

Different? I say, and there is a moment then, the two of us, her and me, where we are breathing at the same time and I sense, in a way I have never sensed before with any Author, that we are together.

Yes, she whispers. What if it's different with, or different without, and all of us are different anyhow, and I am different here on my own, different in my aloneness and my contentment, without the other-halves that they all talk about, the my-sons, my-daughters, it's me, not "just" me, me, in myself and my difference.

Tell me, I say. Go on.

GUIDANCE SUBJECTS

Please see the links below for guidance and downloads on a range of subjects and issues:

- Baby and Infant Funerals – Policy and Guidance
- Body Parts
- BRAMM: British Register of Accredited Memorial Masons
- Charter for the Bereaved
- Environmental
- Foetal Remains Policy and Baby and Infant Cremation
- Health and Safety
- Holding Over Cremations

Burn me, what do I need this body for

- Legislation
- Management of Memorials
- Mercury and Emissions
- Pandemic Planning
- PI Questionnaires
- Recycling Floral Tributes
- Recycling of Metals
- Reuse of Graves
- Transfer of Rights
- VAT on Funerals

> "Women have always had to be amphibious. No society has been designed for their comfort or convenience, and as they move between the elements, the spheres of private and public, personal and professional, they must constantly adapt, assume disguise, or camouflage."

Yesterday, and last week, I wore it: the new top, the plunge of it, the exposure of it. Last week I wore it alone and oh the plunge of it, the exposure of it. Not smart or fancy, simple cotton but there they were, when I looked down, and I imagined there they were to everyone who saw. No one said. I was aware when I bent over, and partly thrilled. I bent over and thought, This is more of me outside than usual, here is more of me, the woman part of me, does this make me woman, womanly, these parts, this show of shine of skin?

Yesterday I added something underneath, to try to lessen the plunge of it, the exposure, and found myself pulling, tugging, rearranging – to lessen or to undo the effect? I don't know. I don't know how I want to be inside and out, to cover or reveal, to whom, to what, and when? Worrying, lightly anxious, now at this age where I am perhaps past it all, where thoughts of attractive… no, it's not that. For me, this is. For me, and am I out there, is this disguise, camouflage, or undisguise? More of traditional, the busty 'here-is-it-all, below my short-short hair, unusual in a gathering of women' look I still have. These. There they are!

> "The department store was a corner of the world that was, unusually, laid out for the convenience of women. The business of Marshall and Snelgrove [on Oxford Street] was to create an environment in which women without male companions could linger, and there were not many such places in the 1920s and 1930s. Clubs were mostly for men, and those for women tended to be austere. A woman, or women, unaccompanied by a man, would not be served at a respectable bar. In a department store, there was a restaurant or cafe. There was also, very importantly, a women's lavatory."

Ah, now this explain my strong call towards it, a department store in this new city I have moved to. I grew up in another city and one of the most famous of department stores, more than 100 years old this year, was almost my local shop, was where we went, although I don't know what we did there.... What did we do there, me and my mother?

I went, a few weeks or months ago, here in this new city, and rose up and up, wandering round that soft, safe world of prices I will never pay, but where I can slip between displays of shoes, imagine myself another. Is that it? Or let myself be without the outside world pressing me. Looked at, or unlooked at, I am not sure now what the problem is, or if there is, in fact, a problem. Everything is laid out, there is a guide to every floor, and there is food inside, and there are, yes, the toilets. All is convenient, expected, and all of them – mostly, women, with perfume sprays, with samples and anti-ageing creams, yes, I am that age – are there to help me. Are there to smooth me. I smile at them. I laugh at the hats, the lunacy of pricings. I am a woman on an escalator, unaccompanied by anyone.

Marjorie Agnes

Can you believe you were in Paris at the beginning of the week? Can you believe you were in Paris at the beginning of the week, alone, walking through the streets? April in Paris? Can you believe that you, a woman on her own, with her own money and no one depending on her, are able to do these things, take yourself off, for April in Paris? Can you believe you can live as a woman, on her own, without having to have a spouse, without having to have children?

Can you believe you were in Paris at the beginning of the week, and on your last day, you sat under a tree in the park, reading the end of Fear of Flying, where she is in Paris, having a revelation?

Are you having experiences just so you can write about them in this—

Am I having experiences just so I can write about them? she asks me. I mean, that's not normal, is it? Tonight I stood in the kitchen, cutting my hair, the back gets so long so quickly, short hair is hard, and it's expensive to keep going to the hairdresser, so I was there, in the dark, I couldn't see, with these huge scissors, cutting the back, who knows what it looks like. And I was thinking as I was cutting, how I would write about it. This is new, she says. Me watching myself do things. I mean, I've mostly written fiction before, so this wasn't an issue. Yes, I've been writing poetry, but it feels different… this feels different. Poetry has a shape, I form it, make it neater, but this is like a lump of clay that I'm poking a little, without a plan, without a this-will-be-a-pot, or a bowl, or a plate. So: What if I am?

What if you are having experiences just so you can write about them? I say.

Yes, she says. I mean, doesn't that seem, I don't know, inauthentic?

I believe many Authors do this, I say. But more importantly: who is judging you? Who is going to know? After you finish the book, who will know what you did and what your reasons for doing it were? Part of this book is fiction, isn't it?

Definitely, she says. I haven't been to a town full of angry women. Although I think I live in a town full of angry women, who doesn't! A world full of angry women!

I hear her laughing.

I'm reading about the suffragettes, she says, and that does make me angry. I hadn't understood. I thought it was about voting. I feel like an idiot.

Why?

I never really thought about it, she says. I'm pretty intelligent, I read a lot, and I never really imagined how it might be to live in a country ruled entirely by men, where no one in power looked like you at all. Where you and those who were like you had so little say, almost none. It's not about democracy, is it? I mean, not all men even had the vote a hundred years ago, did they?

What is it about? To you, I mean.

I was reading the memoirs of one of the leading women in the suffragette movement, Emmeline Pankhurst. It was written, or at least published, in 1914, before some women did finally get the vote, in 1918. And what struck me...

There's silence here and I wonder if I should say something.

She coughs. I wait.

What struck me, she says, with a small laugh, is what she said about seeing. What women see that she thought men, especially the men in power, don't. And if they do see, they don't care. Women in the workhouses, girls with illegitimate children. She saw these women, these girls. For the men in power, this wasn't even a problem: how an elderly woman is fine while her elderly husband is alive, they have his pension. But she writes that his pension dies with him – what a phrase, Emmeline repeats it several times, "His pension dies with him" – and the wife, the widow? To the workhouse. This is what happened to women. And this is what only a woman could see.

Do you think some men would want to be shown, I say, how to see this way?

It's hard, she says, because I don't like, or I never did like, to see the genders like this, women one way, men another. I don't believe in the "different brains" argument, I've read enough to show that science can't prove it. But society teaches us how to see, no? I read an article recently, a science article, that says that we don't even really see what's in front of us – our brains come up with an estimate, a prediction of what we are likely to see, and adjust accordingly.

Gosh, I say. That's fascinating.

Isn't it? We're always filtering, our brain is trying to fit the world into our idea of the world. Confirmation bias – we look for evidence that supports what we already think. I find this quite horrifying. I don't want to think of myself this way. I want to imagine myself as open to new experiences, as reacting spontaneously as something occurs, without any bias. I don't suppose that's true though, do you?

I don't know, I say, and I am starting to wonder what I think about everything she is presenting me with. Do I have a prediction about how an "Author" should be, and am I adjusting myself to her, trying to make her fit? I'm sorry, I say, I don't think I am being particularly helpful.

Oh no, you are! she says. This book, this thing, is evolving, is happening to me now, is being "happened" by me right now, it feels so raw and so instantaneous, and you are helping a great deal. You're helping by not stopping me. You are helping by not saying, Wait, a book doesn't normally look like *this.* You aren't saying, Shouldn't you have a coherent story, shouldn't you know by now what's happening?

No, I say. I don't believe it's my role to say those things.

Thank you, she says. See how much you are helping!

My role is to say, 'go on', I say to her, and she is laughing again, and I am laughing.

Go on, she says.

She is asking me for permission, I say to the group when we next meet.

Oh yes, someone says. I understand that. She needs you to validate that she is doing something unique, otherwise why would she bother.

Does this always happen? I ask, as we sit around the table. We have been discussing one Narrator's issues with an Author working on the third book in a trilogy, and how my friend is gently attempting to steer their Author from including everything from the first two books to "make sure" a new reader won't be confused. It's so long! my friend kept saying to us. It's over a thousand pages! Won't an editor deal with that later? one of the most experienced of us suggested, and my friend nodded, said yes, probably and that there wasn't much to be done anyway. This Author's first two books had been great successes and so the Author wasn't very open to a Narrator's input. It makes an easier life for me, I suppose, says my friend. At least your Author is interesting!

That's true, I say. She has never done anything like this before and it is fascinating what she worries about. She really shouldn't worry about anything, though. What she writes, how she writes. I don't doubt it will coalesce.

Such a lovely word, sighs one of the others, who always prefers to work with poets.

At least you're not concerned, says another to me. You can be her rock. That seems to be what she needs, a steady voice telling her to...

...Go on, we say in a chorus and we laugh. We have been well trained. Someone gets another round of drinks.

Gladys May Gordon

"Ladylike," she says to the dead. The cemetery today is full of daffodils. It is a rare day of sunshine, a rare April day. "Ladylike," she says, sitting on a bench, with gravestones in front of her and behind. "I don't know what that means. I don't know what that meant. Do you know about the suffragettes, have you heard of all this? Were some of you...?"

Yes, some of them, men and women – and the children, there are children here too, laughing – have heard. A few were there, this was their time, and you might think the men were one way and the women another. But there are men who weren't that way, men who were excited, delighted; men who knew women, really knew women, and from what they knew of other men, wanted the women instead. Men who had to, were forced to, spend so much time with these other men, this type of man, this blustering, this so loud, this very much shouting and we-are-in-control man, and wanted – if they had been that type – to punch this man, these men, to stop up the mouths of these men. They, some men, wanted to hear the women's voices, wanted everywhere to be filled instead with the voices of women.

The women who know, who were there, in the before and the during and the coming after, did not always have men who were their champions. They want to say to the woman sitting in the sunshine on the bench, with daffodils, to keep talking, keep her voice going, not shut it inside. They wonder as they listen to her – she is talking now about public toilets, how she hadn't realised what a difference, oh my god, with all those long skirts and being out of the house, what a woman might need that wasn't there! – whether she is like this everywhere. They understand that the cemetery, although it is their world, is not The World, and that their friend who walks, who talks to them, reads them poetry, comes and goes, can come. And go.

Where is her outside? some of them whisper to each other. What does she have? Who looks after her? But inside themselves they suspect, they hope and thrill to it, that no one looks after her at all, because looking-after means keeping in, means "ladylike", means no-you-can't, even if it is said with honey, even if it is woman to woman, even if it's said with love.

"I thought," their friend on the bench is saying now, "that really it was only about votes. I feel like an idiot. It was yesterday; it was in my grandmother's time, she's dead now... Oh dear, I'm sorry, should I not...?"

She stops, as if listening, as if they need to give her permission. We are not bothered, they tell her, don't mind mentioning of death and dead, we are what we are now and what we were is not, and it is what most people in the world are. We outnumber you, so please, please speak. She does.

"Not about the vote, I mean. These women who might have been my grandmother, I can't imagine her not being able, being told she can't. She was so..."

She stops again, and this time the dead see she is realising, and they wait. This woman, they see, is here because of the realising, she comes here to open up that space for herself, she talks to them to help it open. Look, they say to each other, the men too, and the children. Look, she is getting something, she is taking something new and trying it inside her head. They watch the woman as she adds something to her self.

Go on, say the dead.

Florence Dunn

After reading the article, the first one I hired was a Fake Mother for £50 an hour. The article, which had been about companies that provide fake relatives in Japan, had left me reeling – confused, I think, but also with this sudden longing. I had to find out; I felt I had to try it.

I spent a while wondering if I should rent a Fake Mother who looked a lot like my real one, or would it be better if she was nothing like her? In the end, I went for something in between: the Fake Mother would also have blonde hair, but would be a bit taller and slightly younger.

Of course, I was hoping that the Fake Mother would be entirely different, in the way that mattered.

I didn't give them, the company, any guidance about what I wanted her to say to me, how I wanted her to behave. It seemed they didn't need any. That when you tick the "Mother" box, there are assumptions. What I wanted to know was whether hearing those things, from a complete stranger I was paying to tell me, would do... something.

We would meet in town. We would go shopping. This was not something the real one and I had ever done. (We did, yes, once or twice, and it was fraught, involving buying me shoes, which I hated. Or some end-of-season sale scrum, with racks and racks of No Wonder No One Bought These Full Price.) I was early; I waited under the clock. I was nervous. I would say it was like a date, but I hadn't really ever had any of those either. This was entirely its own brand of nervousness.

While I waited, I thought about the last time I met up with my real mother. I hadn't wanted to, but it had been a year since the two of us had last spent time, and I felt I should. I worked myself into quite a state beforehand, but I had had a very odd experience during the short hour she and I sat in a strange little cafe together. For the first time, I felt as though I were sitting opposite not someone I was related to but an elderly woman, one who had known me as a child, an old woman who wanted someone to talk to, to listen while she spoke critically about one person after another, a list of complaints. You are nothing to do with me, I thought, and the thought disturbed and relieved me.

If my real mother was like a stranger, then why, I thought, shouldn't a stranger be ...?

I noticed a woman walking towards me. This woman was smiling, she had been given my photo, she knew who I was, and she approached me with complete certainty, certainty that comes from knowing someone for their whole life. The certainty that comes with giving birth to that person. She didn't give me a moment to fumble or stammer. She hugged me. A complete stranger, who I was paying £50 per hour to pretend to be my mother, hugged me.

"You look wonderful," she said, and I realised that I might be about to cry.

We went into the department store and she put her arm through mine. I felt like this was a dream, but although my mother – the real one – often appeared in my dreams, the dream-me was trying to get away from her, or find a way to make her leave my house. This Fake Mother, who thought I looked wonderful, who put her arm through my arm, felt warm. I felt warm.

I don't want to carry on with that, she says.

Okay, I say.

I mean, I don't want to write about that anymore.

It's fine, I say. You don't have to.

But it was such a good idea! she says. I mean, I was going to write all about the Fake Mother and all sorts of other Fake People, and of course the whole thing was fake, it was fiction, but some of it wasn't, the part about mother stuff, and I don't want to go there. Not again. I've done that, you see, I've worked that through, well, can you ever work it all through, but I don't want to go back to it, I don't want this to be about that. Oh dear.

It's fine, I say again, you really don't have to write it. You started. You tried, but if it's not working.

But it's such a good idea! Isn't it wrong of me to abandon a good idea?

Well, I say carefully, what if it wasn't your good idea but an idea that someone else will write?

Oh, she says. That's very interesting. Do you mean, since I got the idea from that article, that another writer is destined to be the one to run with it? Also, it's pretty obvious, it's not like I was doing something really different, it's more or less where you'd go if you read that article and you were a fiction writer.

There is a theory, I say, but I stop because we have been cautioned to avoid theory when in discussions with our Authors. It is a risk that they take in a theory and either stick rigidly to its predictions or become unable to continue, paralysed by abstractions.

A theory about ideas? she says.

It's something some of us talk about, I say. Ideas are out there, waiting to be captured.

And if one writer captures an idea she'll do it her way, and if another writer does, he'll do it differently and it's about who happens to be passing at that moment, who opens up that space you need in your head for an idea to catch? I like that.

Yes, I say. So it may be that you opened up space but this idea turned out not to be for you at all.

You don't think because I snagged it, someone else can't?

Oh no. An idea doesn't vanish when one person is attempting to write it.

Oh good, she says. I feel so relieved, that I don't have to write about it, my real mother or the fake mother, which would involve writing about all that shit, the mothering, the not-mothering, et cetera... Oh god, so relieved that I don't have to!

You never have to, I say. It's your choice.
Yes, she says, sighing. I do keep forgetting that.

There are fewer of us gathering today, the weather is foul, and one of us is enmeshed in a complicated situation of Author illness, says it's "touch and go". The Author is desperate to finish her manuscript before the end, but our friend is worried, of course, that in rushing it she will undo what has come before. It's a tragedy, an Unfinished Book, but the Hurriedly Completed Book can also be a disaster.

Death, we say, sitting round our drinks in a quiet corner. We raise our glasses to the living and sit in silence for a while. I am contemplating the death of characters, and whether it is death if they were never fully alive.

...But they are alive to our Authors, I say, and the others turn and stare at me. Someone laughs.

Are you alright? they ask me. I am embarrassed to have spoken out loud.

Characters, I say, and take a long drink. I was wondering whether the death of a fictional character is comparable to the death of ...

An Author? A real person?

Plants die, says someone. Trees die. They are not people.

But they breathe, I say.

You can have the death of an idea, I believe, says someone else. The death of a scientific theory, when it is disproven by experiment. Neither of those breathed.

That's true, I say.

Ah, the death of truth! says the most voluble of our group, who also tends to be the greatest drinker.

Yes! I say. So, we agree, that the death of a character is a true death? Or a kind of death?

Never agree! says my loud friend, who, I know, is saying it only to disagree.

Everyone laughs, and someone suggests we kill one of us to see what might happen. This provokes great hilarity because we cannot, as you know. Well, you may not know, but this is not the time to elaborate. We are what we are.

In the cemetery, the dead are listening. A number of them, the parents among them, were interested in the story of the Fake Mother. Fascinated. The oldest of them remembers a time when a newborn, if there were already many children, might be handed over to another woman, sometimes related, sometimes not, and that child might never know. This is how it has always been. Money changed hands here too: for the upkeep, and for the secrecy. The modern people, the breathing ones, they think they are so new, they think they innovate. But this is how it has always been. New variants, yes, but not so many entirely unique ideas.

Several of the dead mothers wanted the story to continue. They wanted her to feel warm, to feel warmer, to feel better. Perhaps, they say to each other, when she is feeling stronger, she will carry on telling it. They remember warm. They remember.

[DELETED]

Sarah Ann Chadwick, Mary Ann Chadwick, and **Marion Rogers**

"It's unusual, you know," says the woman sitting next to their grave. "Three buried together, no men. It's definitely different."

Sarah, Mary and Marion laugh.

"We know," says one of them, the woman isn't sure which one. She is sitting by their gravestone in the May sunshine. The cemetery is so beautiful today, full of flowers. They are not sure what she wants from them but it has been some time since one of her type has come.

"We had no children," says one of them, "so there was space for all of us."

"Did you want...?" the woman says. There is more laughing, and the laughing in a cemetery when it comes from the inhabitants of the cemetery is a sound that weaves its way down rows, under and through to almost every corner, every stone, and sometimes, if it is strong, and the wind moves a certain speed, lifts treewards.

"Oh no!" they all say together, and then she can't quite hear who is saying what as there is talking about messiness and crying and the asking of childish questions and the pulling on sleeves and the time it takes, the attention and the screaming, the not-sleeping and the worrying.

"We didn't worry," says the one with the deepest voice, which the woman takes to be Sarah, only because she was the oldest when she died, but the woman does not know how that works now.

"You didn't worry about anything?"

"I mean, we didn't have those worries we saw on the faces of our friends."

"Worries with the husbands!" says the one with the voice that always sounds like there is a joke, and which the woman thinks is Marion, Beloved Niece.

"Oh goodness," says the third voice. "Husbands caused such worry even though they were sometimes delightful..."

"Sometimes!" say the other two together, and there is giggling.

"Did you never want...?" the woman asks, not wishing to offend in any way but also, now that there is this, as she sits by their unusual shared female gravestone – now she has Sarah, Mary and Marion's attention – she wants to know.

"Is anything better than a sister?" says the one the woman thinks is Mary. "She and I, we thought one day we would both find someone who was better than a sister, but we were so happy and getting happier, and after a certain point we knew."

"That no one could ever," says Sarah.

"And then we received Marion!" they say together. "And she was a gift, a gift."

"I had certain issues," says Marion, "which rendered me incompatible with..."

"We took you!' says Mary. 'We wanted you, and there we were, the three of us."

"So happy," says Marion. "I don't believe anyone could have been more."

They sit quietly, four women, only one of them breathing in the world, feeling sunshine.

The woman sitting by the grave wants them to say something more, but she is not sure. She tries to think up a question. Then Sarah speaks.

"We gave each other permission to not do those things that everyone was doing, had always done. Although the times, as well. The war. You know about the war?"

"Yes," says the woman. "Of course. Both wars and one so quickly after."

"Everything changed," says Marion. "We had no idea. Suddenly there were so many of us."

"So many women," says Mary. "Everywhere you went, women were doing what only men had done."

"Marion worked on the buses!" one of them, Sarah or Mary, says. "You should have seen her in her uniform!"

"Collecting tickets," says Marion. "Learning how to sway along the bus, holding on as it took the corner too fast. Always too fast."

"I shouldn't say this," says Sarah, "with all that happened, but in some ways that was..."

"Glorious," says Marion.

"A relief," says Mary.

"All women!" the three say together, and they laugh again.

I can take it out? she says. I can delete that page?

Of course, I say. It is your work, your choice.

Oh thank goodness, she says and I hear the relief, she has distressed herself with the writing and she needs me to tell her.

You needed to write it, I say.

I did, she says. I did. Right then I did.

And now, or later, when you have reached the end...

I wonder if I will ever get there, she says.

I think that is a common feeling, I say.

I can't see it. I don't know if it will exist. But also, I don't know if I want there to be an end, for an end to come, for this to stop. I love this, I think. I love the existence of this, to open it up on my computer, the new page waiting for whatever I want to put on it, it's only been five months and already I am worrying about what happens if I'm without it.

But it's your choice, I say, hoping that I can help her. You can choose not to stop.

I worry about that too, she says, and she laughs and I know she knows that this is sounding a little crazy.

Go on, I say.

- I do not have to be a mother
- I do not have to be a mother figure
- I do not have to be a wife or partner
- I do not have to make your bed
- I do not have to make my bed
- I do not have to go outside
- I do not have to stay at home
- I do not have to talk to one person
- I do not have to talk to many people
- I do not have to be quiet
- I do not have to educate, inform, or entertain
- I do not have to sew labels in school uniforms or make lunch
- I do not have to eat a proper meal
- I do not have to explain why I do not have to do these things
- I do not have to stay silent about why I do not have to do these things
- I do not have to wear a ring
- I do not have to name things
- I do not have to hold a hand
- I do not have to grow my hair
- I do not have to live with a person
- I do not have to not live with my cat
- I do not have to be lonely with someone else
- I do not have to be lonely on my own

> "This book is dedicated to LILLIAN, who lives with nobody but a colony of New York roaches, whose energy has never failed despite her anxieties and her asthma and her overweight, who is always interested in everybody, often angry, sometimes bitchy, but always involved. Lillian the abundant, the golden, the eloquent, the well and badly loved; Lillian the beautiful who thinks she is ugly, Lillian the indefatigable who thinks she is always tired."

This is from the dedication page of The Female Eunuch *by Germaine Greer, Paladin, 1971. Fuck me. I haven't even got to page one and already I am floored, bowled over, almost in tears. I would have loved to meet Lillian, I wonder if anyone I know is a Lillian, but I really know so few people, women, who live alone. I wonder what Lillian thought of that dedication, to be described so candidly, it seems. I put the book down, make another coffee, thinking how I might have felt if someone had dedicated a book to me in this way, me overweight, perhaps badly-loved, and yes, thinking I am ugly. Some kind of epitaph! Would you put this on a tombstone? "Here lies Lillian the abundant, the golden, the eloquent, the well and badly loved; Lillian the beautiful who thinks she is ugly, Lillian the indefatigable who thinks she is always tired." Actually, I think that's beautiful. Oh, Lillian. Oh, Germaine. (11.35am, 19 May 2018)*

Friday ROMAN CATHOLIC PART.

No. 3546 — 30 o'clock p M.

Date May 9. 1924.

Name Ethel Cecilia Walsh.

Age 66 years.

Rank, Trade, or Profession Spinster

Late Residence Union Hospital

District West Didsbury

Mode of Interment Private

Section H.

Number 1688.

Name of Priest, Revd. F. Holt

1924 May 9. Received of

Mr. Board of Guardians

	£	s.	d.
rave Space			
xcavating			
ickwork and Slabs			
s of Slabs			

Ethel Cecilia Walsh *spinster*

When the page is working, you forget there is anything but the page. You forget that beyond the frame of the page, the cat is cleaning itself on a cushion. You forget the pile of books on the sofa arm, waiting to be read. You forget the window. You forget the tree outside the window that yesterday was so severely pruned. You forget yesterday, the day of trees being pruned. You don't see the bookshelves just to the right of the page. You don't see your hands that hold the page. When the page is working, there is no page.

I cried, she says. I was watching a film, it's with Meryl Streep, and there are all these scenes where it's her, the only woman in a roomful of men, men in suits, and I could feel it, you know? She's so good, Meryl, she shows you how it is, her body language, and this is 1971, and she kept having to walk into these rooms, full of white men in suits, trying to tell her what to do. But there are these two scenes where there's a group of women, you have no idea who they are, she walks through them, and they're not referred to, they're not part of the plot, but I had this sense.

It was beautiful, she says. A sense that this was a surreal way that Spielberg found to tell us that our main character – this was based on a true story – inspired other women, she paved the way. The first time this happened in the film, it was sort of mysterious, I wondered who they were, what was going on. The second time, she's walking down the steps of the court house and then suddenly she is moving through this cluster of women, different ages, smiling women. And I cried. Not one tear, you know, but an instant choking up, full-on. And it's so strange, that it's all hitting me, where have I been for 47 years, why hasn't it come to me until now, is it because of what's happening in the world, or was I not looking, off in my little fictional fantasies? And this film, made by a man, and yes, it was a little heavy-handed, but good, she says and she's almost shouting this. Good! It's about time, isn't it? It's about fucking time!

Go on, I say.

From *Other Minds: The Octopus and the Evolution of Intelligent Life,* by Peter Godfrey-Smith, 2017:

the idiosyncrasies of the octopus

quiet lives of very limited mobility

have lost their shells entirely, soft-bodied, unprotected

almost no hard parts at all, it can squeeze through a hole the size of its eyeball and transform its body shape almost indefinitely

a body of pure possibility

the assumption that all animals of a given species (and perhaps of a given sex) will be very similar until they encounter different rewards

the octopuses eye each other from their dens among the shells

"I am angry," says the woman, sitting by the gravestones. "I am so angry, so many things make me angry. Is it me? Should I try not to be like this? Am I letting it all get to me, and 'it all' is really not worth it? Or should I be angry, be angrier? I always thought..."

The dead lean closer: what is she saying? what is she angry about? The dead remember angry, most of them, everyone was once, whatever age, before they came here. Some of them fought, some of them were the violent ones, yes mostly men but also not just, and not just coming to blows, not only blood and bruises but also words and words thrown between them and friends and wives and husbands, children, mothers, fathers, all or most dead now too. Does the rage die, the dead wonder, when we do?

The woman hasn't said anything about what is making her angry. Some of the women think to themselves, It is a man? It must be a man. Some of the women are thinking it is about the woman's mother, they know this, having been, both sides of it, both sides. Or children, but they suspect their woman has none. The way she wants to find the stones of women alone, women unhusbanded, free from the blessing of reproduction. They have heard her say this, seen her write in her notebook, the excitement when she finds another stone with only women, no beloveds, no loving mother loving wife grandmother etc.. They listen to her: "I know I will probably never know," she whispers to those dead, "whether you really were. If you were like me, how you lived. But there's a chance, and so I'll say your names." The dead enjoy her naming, her louding them into the air. The dead enjoy her walking, her conversations with them, her attention and her time.

"I am so angry about why everything is still like this," the woman says suddenly. "about why women still have to, about why men are the main, about why we and why it matters. Oh dear."

The woman pulls at her hair, which is so very short that some of the dead when she first arrived thought she wasn't. She is so upset.

"My friend," the woman whispers. "There is a man, a man she says she loves. And she is this brilliant woman, she is brilliant in every way, and tough, tougher than me, like me in parts but better. And her man tries to hold her tightly, turn her so her face shines only on him, tries to change what she wears and says and does. And I want to kill him. To kill him for not letting her be everything she is."

"Oh no," she says, "I'm sorry, I'm sorry, you know I don't really mean that..."

The dead don't mind the talk like this, after all, they know what 'dead' means and some of them wonder if she could not do worse to this man, the love of her friend who holds too tight? Worse things when he is living, no, than bringing him to them?

When the woman cries, the dead think they would hold their breaths if they still could and they would comfort her if they had a way, and they hope that the woman can feel them and their helpingness around her. She must like it where they are, she keeps coming. The dead who are watching and listening to the woman look at each other, concentrating, wishing they could do for her what she does for them with her walking, her talking, her naming. The dead wish this as hard as they can, while the woman sits, pulls at her hair, and cries.

ELIZABETH MORVILLE
ELLEN MORVILLE HALL

In
Loving Memory of
ELIZABETH REBECCA FROST
(CISSIE)
DIED FEBRUARY
ALSO KATE
DIED MARCH 12TH
ALSO LILLY
DIED DECEMBER

IN LOVING MEMORY OF
WHO DIED DEC
MARY JANE RUSSELL
WHO DIED FEB
AGED 72 YEARS
WHO DIED FEB

I keep thinking, she says during our next conversation, about the article on the girl in that fugue state, do you remember?

I do, I say. It wasn't so long ago when you wrote it. What does it make you think of?

Oh so many things, she says, and I hear her sighing. I have become used to her sighing during our conversations. It doesn't put me off… it is a mannerism, part of her thinking process, part of her writing process.

I think, she says, that I wonder if we are all in some kind of fugue state, or rather, if I am, at least some of the time? If it's about losing your sense of self, don't I do that when I am writing my characters, or even when I am writing in something that sounds like my own voice? Or maybe we can never be in a fugue state because you have to assume first that there is some fixed state of ourselves, some identity or self we could somehow lose in a fugue.

Yes, I say. It's a very interesting point. Is there a self to be lost?

I was talking to a friend today, she says, and it's always a risk, telling someone else the oddness that's in your own head, the thing you think you must surely be the only one thinking. But the joy when she said it's the same for her, when I told her that if I don't see her or one of the others I feel closest to for around two weeks, I start to lose my sense of myself. And she said, Yes! And she said about people reflecting back to you who you are, which is exactly what I meant. I said how I didn't have that for a long time, and I could feel, when weeks went by without being truly seen by anyone, as if small bits were falling off me, as if my self was flaking. Are we all at risk, if we are unseen for too long, are we always on the edge of fugue?

I don't answer her straight away, I am so taken with that phrase, "edge of fugue", and am making sure to remember it to tell the others next time. My Author, it feels she is getting to the heart of something now.

I'm getting to the heart of something now, she says, and I am startled.

Yes, I say. You are. Go on.

Edge of fugue, I say. We are sitting in our usual corner, discussing work, which is our lives, of course, there is so little else. Isn't that a wonderful phrase!

What does it mean? says one of the other Narrators.

I am not sure, I say. We are at some point in this where she is, I do feel she is, getting somewhere. She said this and I thought it best not to push. Something about selves, the self, more than one self inside. She wrote about an article she read, a missing girl, they thought she entered a fugue state, lost herself.

How interesting, says someone else. Is she thinking about her characters as if they are other selves inside her?

She might be, I say. Although I think she has always seen herself as not having such a fixed self herself.

Self herself! We laugh, the crisps are passed around.

I'm glad we don't have to worry about these things, or only for them, says my friend whose dying Author is managing, somehow, to still be writing. We have enough to worry about without these...

...existential concerns, says one of us who appreciates long words.

Are you worried about her? someone asks me. That she might not...?

Oh no, I say. And I'm not. She is writing. She is thinking about writing, she is allowing herself to move to interesting places. I believe all is going well. I am now simply required to listen and nudge occasionally.

Listen and nudge," the others murmur. Yes. Yes.

It is my birthday and on my birthday I do not have to   at all

It is my birthday and on my birthday I do not feel too old too young

It is my birthday and I have never felt this feeling of lack of feeling before   no worries nothing
in my stomach   no edge of anything   no wanting different
how odd how odd how odd

It is my birthday and I am thinking of everything I have done and I have done and I have done and I have written and written and laughed   there has been so much laughing recently oh yes and thinking of all the laughing makes me cry
I'm happy   on my birthday on my own

the cat is in the wardrobe   wonderful company and messages from people

writing writing writing

We left the baby in the forest. We wanted to see what might occur. We had pre-installed the cameras, with the trees' permission. You can't do it without their go-ahead, we learned. Technology becomes a tangle of well-placed leaves, the images – if any are captured at all, what with all the damp – are vague and unconstituted. The trees need to be on your side. We left the baby and we waited.

I watch a documentary, *Bombshell*, about Hedy Lamarr. She had seven husbands, but she says she never felt seen beyond her face. She never felt properly loved.

She was not only a film star but also an inventor: she invented frequency hopping, the technology behind WiFi, GPS.

Which enabled the Allies to control their torpedoes remotely.

Husbands

Frequency

Torpedoes

We leave the baby in the forest. We want to see what might occur. We have pre-installed the cameras, with the trees' permission. You can't do it without their go-ahead, we learned. Technology becomes a tangle of well-placed leaves, the images – if any are captured, what with all the damp – are vague and unconstituted. The trees need to be on your side.

We leave the baby and we wait.

The first mother doesn't understand what she is seeing. She stares at our screens.

"It's a baby," we say, to prod her to respond. The first mother leans closer to the screen. "A baby in a forest," we say kindly, helpfully.

"What?" says the first mother. "What is...?"

We are filming her too, of course, filming her watching the live feed of the baby that we have left in the forest. Right now, it is around noon in the forest, which is not in fact too far away from where we are, in the room with the screen and our cameras and our first mother. The baby is lying where we left it, staring up into the leaves. The baby appears fine (we have, of course, rated the baby based on an extensive list of criteria, which we reassess on an hourly basis. We are rigorous. The Ethics Committee demanded it.)

"A baby," she says, and we record that her first use of the word "baby" occurred at seven minutes into the session. "Why is there a...?"

Our carefully designed protocol means that we only offer restricted information and we leave the mothers – of whom this is the first – space to provide their own interpretations.

"The baby has been left there," we say.

"You left a baby? In a forest? Alone?" says the first mother and we record how the pitch of her voice is rising. Later, we will examine the data on increase or decrease in skin conductance and other measures of anxiety, stress and fear.

"Yes," we say.

"Oh god," moans the woman. She lifts one hand up to cover her mouth.

"Do you think the baby is in any danger," we read from our list of questions. The woman stares at us now rather than the screen.

"You're all fucking crazy," she mutters.

"If this was your baby," we begin to say, but the woman stands up and starts to rip our sensors off her arms and temples.

"Fuck it," says the first mother. "I don't care what you're paying me. I'm not fucking doing this." She grabs her handbag from underneath the chair, heads to the door and then she looks at the screen again and shakes her head. We think she murmurs something like "for fuck's sake". We write it all down.

Although this session has ended prematurely, we are not unpleased that a reaction has been provoked, and this is only the first mother. We restore the room to order, place our clipboards neatly back into the box, check on the status of the baby, and move towards the coffee room.

I am making me a book, she says. It's all for me! I think I knew that from the start but wasn't sure. Or wasn't sure I should be. Wasn't sure a book could be allowed to be for its author.

Why not? I say. Who is allowing or not allowing?

That's a great question, she says. She sounds immensely happy, I am not sure I have ever heard this in her voice. We are on page 85 and she is clearly delighted. So I am delighted. I am also thinking about my previous conversation with her, and wondering if this is a new self, Delighted Author, or a delighted version of her previous self. I am finding myself a little sidetracked but do not mention this. I am here to listen, nudge and encourage… not to steer.

I don't care anymore, I think that's it! she says. I'm enjoying myself so much, who cares if this is a book written for one person? How much better does it get than that? Oh, I've just remembered, I wrote a short story a few years ago...

Go on, I say.

It was called *The Most New Sport* or something like that, and it was about two friends who invented a game and tried to persuade people to play it. They wanted it to catch on, like football or baseball. They wanted everyone playing it.

I imagine that's what has happened before, I say. With tennis and all the other sports. Someone had to invent them, teach people the rules, hope that it would take.

Yes! she says. But in my story the two inventors discover that no one else can understand their sport except them. It's too complicated, they're told. People give up easily, and the investors they're trying to woo aren't interested. And so they accept that they've invented a sport that only they can play, want to play. So they play, just the two of them.

Oh how interesting, I say. I imagine this might have happened too, throughout history.

I was surprised, she says, I didn't predict that the story, which is very short, a page or two, would go that way, but the best things I've written don't go the way I think they will. And I learn from my own stories. I wrote that one years ago, during a trip to America when the Olympics were on, I think, and I saw an awards ceremony on a TV screen while I was getting coffee. That sparked it. But I see now that it was telling me, my own story, that it's fine to create something that will never have mass appeal – or even appeal to anyone besides myself. Creation, creativity, it's the doing of it.

It appeals to me, I say, and immediately wonder if I should have said that. Is that judgemental, steering? No, it's probably encouraging. Nudging.

Thank you, she says. I'm glad, although I don't really care. I hope you don't mind me saying that, but I really don't. Fuck it. Not you, of course. I mean, Fuck the notion that I am supposed to please anyone with this. I am enjoying it. I AM ENJOYING IT!

Wonderful! I say. That's wonderful!

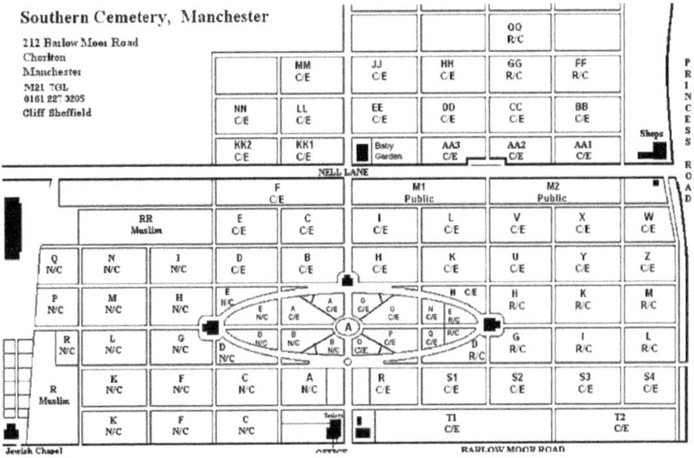

Southern Cemetery, Manchester

212 Barlow Moor Road
Chorlton
Manchester
M21 7GL
0161 227 3205
Cliff Sheffield

C/E Church of England
N/C Non- conformist
R/C Roman Catholic

A group of the dead are talking among themselves about the baby left in the forest. They hope that this is not the end of that story, the first mother and her distress, surely there will be more, more mothers, perhaps. Surely a baby cannot simply be left in a forest, even being watched. Some of the dead were great readers in their time, many of the women, and some of them were writers too, although in secret: not for show, not for publication. The readers among the dead understand the idea of a fiction, of imaginings, and that it can be as affecting as the truest tales. The dead are not sure anymore what true might mean, being here, as they are, fixed in their places, but also unfixed, untimely. They hope the woman will carry on with this, the baby alone, the trees watching. They wait.

It's so odd, she says. I think I've just written the end. It came to me, out of the blue: a line! And then the whole thing, it felt sort of magical, it's been a long time since… you know. And I thought at first what came wasn't for this. I thought it was separate, stand-alone. But I was in the bath and I realised – and this was only a few hours after writing it – that it might be the end. Of this. Of this whole long thing. And so I've put it at the end, after a load of blank pages. Something for Future Me to find or work towards, or to get to and think, Oh god this doesn't fit! I do like thinking of Future Me, but usually in terms of chocolate I've bought which I know, because I'm at that age, I will forget completely and the Me-of-Tomorrow will get this lovely surprise, Oh look, chocolate! And she'll be grateful to Past Me. I like the idea of making Future Me happy. Of thinking of me then, not now, a time-based me, whatever I may have done by then or even be. I've never placed a piece of writing somewhere for her, though. That's new.

How odd, she says again, this feels like I've been taken over, that amazing feeling when you're not the one doing the writing – but here it's not just that I'm not the one doing the writing, I'm not the one doing the compiling, either, the putting-together of it all. It's being 'happened' to me, which is terrible grammar, I know, but that's how it feels. Wow. Wow. I like it.

Go on, I say.

"I had prepared my defence," says the woman. She is sitting on the grass by the Beseeching Angel With No Hands. "I was sure she would ask me questions about how I'm living. It's crazy," she says, "I had got a whole list together: why I want to live alone, how great it is, why I don't want to be in a relationship, all of it going round and round in my head. And she didn't ask! It's funny, me being so defensive."

The woman stands up and walks towards one of us. "Elizabeth Walburn," the woman says aloud. She has already written this in her book and we have also heard her say: "Elizabeth Ann Armstrong" and "Margaret Roberts" and "June Rosson". She has said all of these out loud and we think it may be not only because of women but because of their aloneness under, their not sharing of their places with anyone here. The woman seems to be surprised by these, and to be looking for these.

"Did this happen to you?" she asks Elizabeth Walburn. The woman stands and waits for a moment. We wait too; we have never heard Elizabeth Walburn speak. "Were you alone?" the woman asks, and we cannot tell if she is sad or delighted or curious or perhaps everything, it is possible to be everything, we know that, we see it. It is possible to be grieving and celebrating a freedom, possible to be happy and lonely sometimes and wanting people and never wanting people. Possible, we know, to not know at all what to want and what not to want. Elizabeth Walburn doesn't say anything: no clearing of a throat, nothing.

We watch the woman walk on towards Margaret Roberts and stand, looking at her stone, her dates. The woman laughs, she often laughs when she comes to us, and we like that sound very much.

"I feel so silly!" she says to Margaret Roberts. "I feel like an idiot, that I would have to defend myself. Or that she was even interested, it might be more that. And it might also be that she didn't want to hear it, my life and how great this is. Or it might be a million other things, I don't know. But I am defensive, I think."

"Silly girl," says Margaret Roberts, who is a talkative one.

"I know," says the woman, kneeling down on the grass. "Why can't I get on with it without thinking about it all?"

"Oh, not to worry about the thinking," says Margaret. "I meant silly for being defensive, silly for worrying. Less time with that is always better. Time – you know you have it – take it."

"Did you?" says the woman.

"Of course not," says Margaret, "or how would I have learned that it's for taking and not wasting? Too soon, it was all over."

"I don't mind dying," says the woman.

"Oh, but you will," says Margaret. The woman cannot see how we all are nodding you will, you will, you will.

Inspector Morse, series 2 episode 2, "Last Seen Wearing", aired 8 March 1988*:

```
Inspector Morse: You live alone?
      PAUSE
Woman (reclining on sofa): Two cats.
```

*watched 14 August 2018
** Five minutes later her character is murdered. We never find out what happens to the cats.

GUIDANCE SUBJECTS

Please see the links below for guidance and downloads on a range of subjects and issues:

- Baby and Infant Funerals – Policy and Guidance

who could who ever could this can't be even with guidance oh dear

- Body Parts
- BRAMM: British Register of Accredited Memorial Masons
- Charter for the Bereaved
- Environmental
- Foetal Remains Policy and Baby and Infant Cremation
- Health & Safety
- Holding Over Cremations
- Legislation
- Management of Memorials
- Mercury & Emissions
- Pandemic Planning
- PI Questionnaires
- Recycling Floral Tributes
- Recycling of Metals
- Reuse of Graves
- Transfer of Rights
- VAT on Funerals

The second mother reacts differently. When we show her the baby in the forest, when we say, “We left the baby in the forest, alone”, she appears unperturbed. She has the same number of children as the first mother, is approximately the same age and socioeconomic background, yet the readings we capture from our sensors as she sits and watches the baby – who is, once again, quite content lying there on the forest floor – show very little elevation.

“This is live, of course?” she says.

“Yes,” we say. We wait.

She sits there for a while. Then she turns to us.

“Is there something I am supposed to do?” she says. “Or say?”

“Is there something you would like to do or say?” we ask. We are attempting not to steer the participants in any direction.

“No,” she says. “Not really.”

We leave it another five minutes in order to reach our minimum participation duration, and then we remove her sensors and she leaves.

The childless woman’s reaction is more shocking. We had not wanted to label this cohort “childless”, there had been several disagreements, and “child-free” had been mooted, but we had been unable to agree on a more suitable word, so this was our designation. A similar age to the mothers, but without children: that was our second target population. We had made assumptions. We had a theory, of course. But we were not prepared for this.

Within sixty seconds of being seated in front of the live feed of the baby, she began to cry. We decided later that the word “crying” was simply inadequate. Sobbing, wailing, it involved her entire body and a great quantity of tears and volume of sound. The baby, as usual, was contented and staring up at the leaves, so it was not a reaction to a distressful image. Or any more distressing than simply the sight of a baby, alone, in a forest.

We offered her tissues when the cacophony began to diminish. A few minutes later, when the worst seemed to have subsided, we asked questions.

“Could you tell us,” we said, “ what provoked your reaction?” We were careful not to use a word such as “extreme”, so that she did not feel she was in any way unusual. Although, of course, she was, and later we would admit to each other that we had been slightly frightened.

She didn't answer us straight away, although she was no longer weeping. Then she said:

"I don't know. I really don't. To be honest" – and here she shifted her chair so she was no longer looking straight at our baby – "I have never had much feeling for babies at all. I never wanted one, like I said on your forms. But this." She waved her hand towards the screen. "I don't know. I don't know at all."

We didn't get much more from her. We waited a while before removing her sensors. As she got up to leave, she walked towards the screen and made as if to reach a hand towards our baby. We watched her, wondering what else she might do, how else she might surprise us. But in the end she did nothing, nodded to us, and left.

We never published our paper. Our results were in disarray, we had no findings at all to speak of, mothers and childless, those with fewer children, those with younger or older offspring, no variables that correlated with anything, whether empathy, sympathy, detachment, hysteria. We packed up our screen and our sensors, and went back to the forest.

The trees seemed disappointed when we retrieved our baby. We thanked them for their careful attention, both to our baby and our video cameras. The video cameras were still intact and functioning, and our baby was still contented, gurgling. We put the baby in its carrier and walked slowly down the same path we had entered by, wondering exactly where in our experimental design we had gone so very, very wrong.

I have so much to say, she says, and it's stopped me from writing anything. Is this a normal stage, you know, in the process, in the book-writing, in this thing?

I think you know what I am going to say, I say, and we laugh.

Yes, she says. There is no normal!

Exactly, I say. It has been nine months now, and we know each other better. I am not concerned when I don't hear from her. I'm not concerned something's going terribly wrong. She seems in excellent spirits.

So much to say, she says and I hear her sighing. I want to put it all down and I also don't want to put it all in there, in case it's too much, in case it's too much for me, first. I just re-read the last few pages, I like it a lot. Is that strange?

I think it's wonderful, I say, and I really do. I have heard from my colleagues no end of stories of manuscripts being torn up, even burnt, when the Author falls into some sort of despair or self-loathing in the middle of the process. I had been steeling myself, but I believe we have passed the Middle now, we are, as they say, on the home stretch. That is the sense I get from her. And she is entirely the opposite of despairing. Her joy is infectious.

I listen to the radio, she says, and I'm watching various films and television programmes, and some are historical, that young woman in the 1950s who goes to Guernsey, her fiancé wants to strap her down, tie her down, the director makes that point quite literally on the airplane. She doesn't want that, although I was disappointed that she had to be paired up at the end. But I know Hollywood, very little imagination about other sorts of happy endings. And a TV drama, 1973, and the sexism, oh god, a young policewoman and it's all about making the tea and laughing and groping. And she kisses him, her boss, and I was hoping there would be none of that, but I do know that's my own issue, the sex thing, the man-and-woman thing. And oh! she says and there's a pause.

Go on, I say.

Well, she says slowly, I am not sure if this fits in, gosh, I didn't think I would mention it, but there was a flirtation last week. I think. A flirtation with a woman. I've never. I don't think I have, I mean. Not this. I think I thought there never would be. With anyone, I mean. It was a particular situation which was. Oh goodness, you can't see, but I'm blushing.

What happened? I say. If you'd like to tell me?

I would, she says. I was staying in a hotel for three nights, with my parents. This is unusual, I almost never stay in hotels, or if I do, it's for work, and it's only a night. But I think it was this, the location and the time span, that there was time for something, only something tiny, to unfold. The woman, she works at the hotel. And I should say, nothing was said. I mean we chatted a tiny bit, she was friendly to everyone. But I had a sense. Of an energy between us, one of those situations where you are aware of the other person in a crowded room, whatever they are doing. And a sense that it might be that for her too. And you see, I had thought I couldn't. Couldn't do this, not only because I am 48 now, but because I didn't have the right machinery for transmitting and receiving these sorts of signals. Really, since I was in my twenties I've thought there was something other people had that was switched off in me.

She pauses.

Go on, I say.

I was pretty upset about this for years, I couldn't figure out how other people did it, this sort of mating dance thing, the flirting, the hooking up. I learned after a while that it wasn't about prettiness, some sort of objective beauty, but about attraction, and it was as if I was the wrong magnet. Or rather, I was a metal that didn't magnetise. I thought of myself like one of those elements, the noble gases, not because I was noble but because they don't react with anything.

I can understand that, I say.

But last week it seemed like I was wrong! she says. Or not wrong, no, but that something has shifted, and where I wasn't able to, didn't have it or it wasn't switched on – well, there was a crackle of electricity, the machinery is there, was woken up! And it was wonderful. I was having a terrible time, my stepmother, my dad, making each other so miserable; I was hardly sleeping, feeling distressed. And this small connection with a stranger, and particularly with a woman, which I've wanted to experience for a long time, made me feel better. Made me feel seen. And seen in a way I'm not sure I've ever felt seen. As almost, you know. Sexual. Attractive.

Go on, I say.

Nothing happened, she says. I thought about something else... more... happening. I enjoyed thinking about it! She laughs. But I didn't need any more to happen in reality than this, a possible spark. It was what it was and it was lovely and it probably kept me sane. And I know I might have been wrong about her side of things, but I think I was probably right because I'm more aware now, I do feel like my sensors have been rebooted. Gosh, all these technology metaphors!

They fit well, I say.

So now I'm thinking about it, looking at myself slightly differently, wondering if a possibility has opened for something else in the future, something I'd shut down. What I'm sure of, she says, and her voice becomes suddenly louder, what I am ABSOLUTELY sure of, is that I don't need it. I don't long for someone else to complete me, make me happy. Nope. I'm fine. More than fine. So contented. I feel relief, it's a huge weight lifted, to be doing this alone, delightfully. I need my friends. I have my friends, all sorts of them, and I feel seen in so many ways by them, they help me be who I want to be in the world. But this, so surprising and delightful. A door opening?

Yes, I say. How wonderful.

Doors, she says. And my choice, if they are opening, what to do. My choice.

Always, I say. Thank you for telling me.

You're the first... I mean, I haven't said anything to anyone! she says. When I started this today, I didn't think I would. It wasn't what was on my mind. Isn't it wonderful, when you start writing, when your fingers start moving and they lead you? They take the lead, and, suddenly, there are doors. Opening.

There is such a boldness to her now, I tell my colleague. There are only the two of us Narrators today, sometimes it is like this; sometimes we prefer it quieter. We are in our corner. It is as if there was a shell and she is cracking it, I say, she is emerging.

Birth, says my colleague. You are easing her out.

She is doing the work, I say, although I admit I am flattered by this description. My colleague pushes the crisps towards me, says with a mouth full: Don't underestimate your role, my friend.

Sorry? I say. My colleague swallows, laughs.

Yes, she could do it without you, of course. We must never imagine ourselves indispensable. But you see her shell, you tap on it, you create gentle fissures, you offer a hand to help her out.

How beautiful, I say. Gentle fissures. And I think again of that phrase my Author used, 'edge of fugue', and whether I am helping her through and across that edge, or assisting her in being comfortable there, which is perhaps where she needs to be to write. I do not tell my colleague, who has gone to purchase another round, that I wonder about myself and how I am affected, feeling myself altered too. We are not supposed to be, or not supposed to think how we might be affected. A midwife might be joyous about every baby that makes it into the world with their assistance, but that does not mean they want to go home with it, watch as it grows. So it is meant to be with us. But I am concerned I will insist on going home with the baby, that I will never want to leave, will have to be prised away. That there may be violence involved.

Cheers! says my colleague, returning with the drinks. I do not say anything about my concerns. I smile.

Cheers! I say.

INT: Living room, night.

A heavy breathing is heard.
Enter an **ANIMAL**. *It is dark. Nothing is seen.*

The animal circles the sofa, which is hundreds of years old. The animal sniffs the right arm, swipes and catches its claw, rips free and leaps onto the table.

On the table is a lamp. The animal switches on the lamp, and sits, cleaning itself.

A second animal enters, stage right.
A third animal enters, stage right.

A faint singing is heard. It is a new version of the oldest song. The animals are still. The sofa does not speak. The lamp is on, is on, is on.

The lamp is switched off. The lamp is switched on and three animals sit on the ancient sofa. The animals are staring at you. The song has finished. One animal begins to read from any book you choose.

You have chosen a book. You have chosen an animal. Here is your armchair. Here is your story.

Listen.

"What amazes me is that she married him in order to change him," she says. The woman is sitting and talking, but not directly to any one of us. Today she has not wandered far, has not written down some of our names or said them aloud. Today she appears less sure of foot: bewildered, we say to each other. "She told me, in front of him," the woman says and shakes her head as if shaking it out, to solve a puzzle and settle her confusion. "She said that she married him because she hoped her love would help him blossom. Blossom! She means: Become entirely not himself."

The woman stands suddenly, holds on to a tree to help.

"She wanted to change him from the start!" she says. We think to ourselves, we women and we men, yes, this is how it sometimes is, it often is. A moulding into, a hope of bringing forth. Whoever she is speaking of, we don't know, but this other she, we want to say, might not have thought of it so. Not so starkly thus, because love – this word excuses very many things. We may be dead but we have not forgotten.

"Twenty-nine years they were married," says the woman, standing more upright now, next to our tree. "That poor man – although, look at the choices he made – did he want to change her too? Maybe he wanted to change her from being a woman who wanted to change him into a woman who accepted him!" She laughs, and we join in. A man she knows and a woman, a wife. Not so strange at all.

"What makes me really sad, though," she says, just as suddenly sitting down again, on the ground by our tree, "is that she still wants it. She says she wants to leave him, but actually she's put him on drugs, antidepressants, and she says if they work – IF THEY WORK! He told me she said that – she'll stay. Doesn't that mean" – and here the woman touches the top of the nearest stone, taps it – "that even after knowing him for twenty-nine years, even after all this time, if he becomes someone different, she won't leave? I'm so angry that she can't care for him, can't let him be. He is a kind person. In the big scheme of men hitting women, of all that awfulness, he is none of that. Can't she see how lucky she is? She blames him for everything. And so he blames himself."

We know this dance, these steps, if not in our own lives then in our sisters', our mothers', our children's. No use blaming, we want to tell her, but we can see she knows. She has been coming here to see us for a while now, we don't know how long because time is not for us. She says twenty-nine years for this man and this woman, has she been here for that long too? Although we think she does not look so older than the first time, so we may be wrong. But she knows about the blaming, the changing, the putting all your happiness on someone else.

"I'm so glad," the woman says, much quieter now, "that I won't be in that place again. I won't let anyone into my head. I look after myself. I look after myself, I always have done. And, you know what? It's a relief, to know that no one will really mind when I die." She leans back against the tree. "I know you tell me I will mind dying, and yes that helps, to be alive right now, I really do want that, but when it happens, and it could be tomorrow or who knows, no one will be distraught. It won't wreck anybody else's life. Because I'm self-contained I don't affect very many people, not directly. There won't be children who regret something they didn't say to me, that we didn't do, who will miss me, or a partner who feels like half of something without me and can't move on. It really is a relief to be out of it. I can't imagine what these two are so scared of that they'd rather be making each other miserable for years and years. Alone is delicious. To be taking on the day, doing what I want, being who I want to be, not bouncing off someone else's idea of me. Delicious."

The woman sits there for a long time, her eyes closed. We haven't said anything today but something we have been has helped her. We did not think that, dead, we could still help. We did not think, dead, that we would be named and talked to.

How to Say 'No'

Inspired by "Re-Writing the Rules", Radio 4, Sept 12th 2018, 11am.

- Start by whispering "I don't think so, sorry" when in a crowded place. To no one.
- When in a slightly less crowded place, say slightly louder, to no one, "I don't think so".
- The next thing you are offered, by anyone, turn it down. No matter if you want it or not. Say "No, thank you".
- When a friend asks you to do something, travel some distance, when they ask you three times to come and you think they must really want you to, don't go. Even if you have agreed, tell them you now can't come.
- When another friend disagrees with you and you are sure the friend is wrong and the friend says, "Don't you see?", say, "No, not really".
- When an invitation comes to work for free or very little money say, "Thank you, but I don't work for free, here is my usual rate".
- When someone tries to pass you a plate of food, even if you want that food, say "No thanks" and pass the plate on.
- When you are asked if you mind about something you do mind about, say "Yes, I do mind. No, I can't let that go, I'm afraid". If in writing, delete "I'm afraid".
- Stand in the middle of your living room and say "no" in your normal voice. Stretch your arms above your head and say "no" in a louder voice. Do this twice a day for a while. Shape your mouth around the no-shape. Find different ways to say it. Say it questioningly, "No?" and firmly, "No!", and settle into your way, your "no", which won't be like anyone else's. This is your own No. Here, have it.

Dr Tania Hershman
@taniahershman

Doing research into women's achievements for @OnThisDayShe, I often see "Devoted to her studies and research, X never married". Her work kept her from doing the "normal" thing? Her singleness helped her work? Hmm. One day, we won't need to mention this at all. #celebratingwomen

9:47 AM · Sep 16, 2018 · Twitter Web Client

* I write this tweet and I want to provoke discussion. But there is only one reply, and it doesn't even seem to address what I was saying. Was what I was saying somehow taboo? I'm wondering this more and more, what we still aren't "allowed" to say, to talk about. Most of my tweets are relentlessly positive, which I understand some people might find annoying, but it's how I choose to be, there, online. Every now and again I post something like the above, to give a bit of insight into me, I suppose, and, I suppose, to try and find a kindred spirit. I didn't find one with this. I also will not find one months later when I post a link to a short essay I wrote, creative non-fiction, something new for me, inspired by *Grey's Anatomy,* the TV show. No one will respond at all, and I will wonder: is it because I say I would be alright to be in hospital alone, I choose to be alone? Is it because I say I like the fact that no one will be distraught when I die, no lives will be torn apart? Am I going against the norms of what we are supposed to want, to say we want? I don't know. I am being very candid for the first time, and I am met by silence. I am a little upset. But I don't regret writing it, I don't regret raising my voice.

It would be annoying, she says, if I fell in love.

Tell me, I say.

Well, I mean, she says, for the book. If I fell in love now, now that I'm writing this book, about a woman, alone in the world, happy and alone, about a happy, alone woman. It would ruin it, wouldn't it?

Why, I say. Something is coming here, I feel. This is a surprise, this turn. She is so interesting, the way her mind works.

Falling in love is so. It's so, I mean. Ordinary. Isn't it? I don't believe it, I think it's manufactured by society, this love thing. This falling in, like it was a pit.

So why are you concerned? I say. Are you concerned it will happen? Or concerned it won't?

She laughs. That's good, she says. You're good. You're good and you're right. Me saying it would be annoying is really me saying, Why hasn't it happened to me? And me saying it's so ordinary is me saying, Why aren't I ordinary? Why am I so strange, so odd, that I have never? That no-one has ever with me? Would I really be so annoyed if, say, next week it came? The love thing. The falling in thing. The thing I don't believe is real. I can say now, while I am not in it and I'm somehow looking forward into a possibility, to some Future Me who is in this "in love", that I would be annoyed because of my book and all the aloneness. But what if, next week or next month, when I am that Future Me, and I am in it, I'm really in it, and I've forgotten all about Past Me, who is me now, and I can't possibly be annoyed from the pit of it? Oh dear, I'm doing my head in. Am I doing your head in? She laughs again and so do I.

A little, I say. I believe you are saying that you can worry now, for Future You, but if it happens to you, when you are Present You, you'll be a different person, you'll be Present-You-in-Love rather than Present-You-Worrying-About-Being-in-Love.

Yes, she says, something like that. And right now I'm worried about this book, I'm Present-Me-Worried-About-Future-Book, but that's not really it, is it?

I don't know, I say. Only you know what it is really.

I'm not sure, she says. Right now, I've been reading Grace Paley, her stories, oh my, and the story about the aunt and all her lovers, and I think I can hear those voices and it's got me started. I wonder about me and where were all my lovers and is it over already? Is it over already at 48? And if it is, what was it and why would I want it anyway. Past Me didn't have so much fun in that regard, I don't think she'd recommend it. If she is sending me any message, it would be: Work on your own heart, stay by yourself, they just mess with your head. And would I be writing this, which I am so enjoying, if I?

Perhaps not, I say.

Even if, she says. Even if there was that, that kind of love, would this book still be? Would there still be that aloneness? This is a part of it, I think, she says. For me, as someone who does think and think and think, and this book is me thinking all the way through and around the thing, the thing I'm in, the thing I want to be in. And I am looking at from in it and also from slightly to the side of it. Maybe that's what being a writer is, that ability to be in and also to be slightly to the side. I've always seen myself as on the edge of every group. My best friend, she's the only one who, when it's more than me and her and we're out walking and I do what I do, I drop back, I daydream and walk more slowly, she is the only one who stops, who turns round, who says, Are you coming? And of course I was testing her, to see if I was seen, because I never was before. Before her. And I do think that if I was seen by her more and more, it might turn from being the most joyous to too much. More's not always better, is it?

Tell me, I say. I can hear her sighing. Edge, I think, but do not say. Edge of fugue, I think.

I don't think I will fall in love, she says. I don't think the book needs to worry about that at all.

Sometimes the women in the town, or two or three of them, are angry at each other.

(Did you think the rage was only about the patriarchy? Did I promise you it would be? Women can be furious with other women too, for things the men, the children, cats and dogs and goats, can't understand.) There is an expectation amongst women that other women will. And when they don't – and they won't because they are human, of course, they misunderstand, they do what they think the other wants but get it wrong, or they do what they want and that is seen as wrong. It's not all sisterly harmony here, or anywhere.

If the set-to coincides with an anger class – and the women involved agree – they may use the classroom to attempt to work it through. Sometimes both will shout, there may be swearing; sometimes one is loud and one is quiet, or both are very calm. Occasionally one woman is extremely upset and the other is instantly contrite and they reconcile. Once or twice, as they argue, the women realise that they are in fact not angry at each other but at a third person, and they discuss how best to resolve that situation.

"It's complicated, isn't it?" says the girl with the short black hair and the nose stud.

"It is," says the instructor.

"Is it because," says the girl, "we can't really see into someone else's head, ever? We will never really know, even if we love them, what someone else is feeling, what someone else wants?"

The girl sitting next to her, who has been chewing her pen, nods and nods at this.

"That's very well put," says the instructor, and the two women who had been angry and who are now sitting quietly, side by side, look at each other. The two formerly angry women smile. One reaches out to touch the other's arm. The class proceeds onto another rage-related topic.

"Emotions such as anger don't necessarily have a fixed effect on behaviour. It may not be necessarily the case that when we're angry, we're aggressive. We may believe that it does... [In the computer game] when people were angry they killed more people in the game than people who were not angry, but only if they believed that anger leads to aggression. Which beautifully shows that we are not puppets on a string. Anger does not make us aggressive without any control on our part."

Maya Tamir, psychology professor, "Oliver Burkeman: Why Are We So Angry?", BBC Radio 4, 17 October 2018

To be alone is to choose exactly the smell of your surroundings

To be alone is to be the one washing, the one cooking, the one putting away

To be alone is to sit and to stand, to move from one room to another, unquestioned, unwatched

To be alone is to be your alone-self, put the outside face on a hook beside the door, with the coats and scarves

To be alone is to choose the music

To be alone is to choose the silence

She is approaching the end, I tell my colleague. I will be very surprised if there is a great deal more. My colleague's Author has just passed away, and my colleague is now a Narrator-in-Waiting and keen to hear how my Author is progressing. We are sitting in a corner, in our usual place.

Ah, says my colleague. There is a shift in tension, isn't there? A feeling in the air, you might say, approaching the end!

Is there anything particular you think I must do? I say.

No, no, let her be. She is in full flow now, she senses it too, believe me, they know. As long as she does not fall into Last Minute Panic, she will finish this. It doesn't matter if she finishes well, that can come later.

Oh, I see, I say. Of course. There are edits, this is only the first draft, after all.

It's the great accomplishment, though. Only after the first draft is born, says my colleague, who has a poetic streak, can it be altered. Only when the whole is there can she see how it is, can she pass it from one hand to the other, feel its weight.

It has been fascinating, being with her through this, a particularly complicated case, no straightforward linearity, I say, and again I do not tell them of my concerns about my self. I hold that back.

You're fortunate, says my colleague. You don't have complicated plot strands to keep track of, characters, tenses, what caused what, et cetera.

No, that's true, I say, although I am concerned. Will it fit? For her it certainly does. But for anyone else? For a reader, say?

Now stop that, says my colleague. Our business is Authors and assisting them in the creation of something as close as possible to what they dreamed of. Or even better. You do worry yourself unnecessarily.

I know, I say. I believe I am going to miss her when this is over.

She will miss you too, says my colleague. I almost say then that I do not want it to end. I almost say something then. I stop myself.

Grand Dame Queenie *Oil on canvas,* 2012 © **Amy Sherald**

SMITHSONIAN NATIONAL MUSEUM OF AFRICAN AMERICAN HISTORY AND CULTURE, WASHINGTON D.C.

COURTESY THE ARTIST AND HAUSER & WIRTH

I am your grandmother, said the grandmother.

We don't think so, we said. We stood on either side, squinting at her. We haven't had you before. How do we know?

Don't I seem like a grandmother? said the grandmother, opening her bag, taking out embroidery.

We looked at each other. This grandmother was correctly small. She had the correct shade and amount of hair. Large bag. Handicrafts. An air of firm kindness. And, of course, the smell of biscuits, though we couldn't be sure what sort.

You do, we said, and one of us consulted our notes. It's just that... But we were unsure what it was just.

Ask questions, children, if you like, said the grandmother, pushing her needle through. She didn't seem at all concerned about our doubt.

We moved away.

I feel like she could be, whispered one of us.

Off, something's off, muttered another.

What's off?

Can't tell. All looks right. Looks right, right?

We agreed she looked right. Too right, perhaps. We went back.

How do you feel, we said, about the war?

Which war, dears? said the grandmother.

Whichever war you prefer.

Oh, I could never prefer a war, said the grandmother, biting the thread and knotting it at the back.

How about... grandfather, said one of us. What was he like? The grandmother smiled, dipped her hand in her bag, brought out photographs.

Your grandfather was a wonderful man, said the grandmother. We peered at the pictures. He looked like a grandfather, one of the young ones, the before-we-came-along ones. We wondered if we remembered him. We wondered if we took turns sitting on his knee, if he gave us pocket money.

Oh, we said. He does look...

I do miss him, said grandmother.

Has it been...?

Oh yes, she said. A very long time. But I have you now, my joys and my delights. Come here, darlings.

Grandmother stood, put down her sewing. She opened her arms. We moved closer. We breathed in that smell. She might be, we thought, as she held us all. And even if she isn't, we thought, closing our eyes.

That was a surprise, she says.

Coming back to that theme? I say.

Yes, she says. I thought I didn't want to, I thought I couldn't. It was the Fake Mother stuff, didn't work for me. But my subconscious...

Ah yes, I say.

... had other ideas! She laughs. A Fake Grandmother. I like it.

So do I, I say. Go on.

"For many offpsring of trauma survivors, they can get it from the parents' post-natal behaviour, just by watching how their parents react to the environment. … People are in control of changing their own biologies, too*. We are not prisoners of the things that have happened in prior generations; we are not prisoners of our genes. Do I still need to be afraid because maybe my parents needed to be afraid? Too much of that will end up holding you back. Our job, if we think we're loaded for vulnerability, we just have to work harder. Knowing this helps, though."

Neuroscientist Dr Rachel Yehuda talking about the idea of inherited fear, in particular in relation to the Holocaust. "Inherited Fear", BBC Radio 4, 18 December 2018

*I had not expected to listen to this programme; I generally avoid anything about the Holocaust, it's too much for me. But I happened to switch it on while I was in the car and then I parked and sat and listened because it was fascinating, talking about emotions, trauma and science. And it made so much sense to me, as the child and grandchild of immigrants, who fled from the Holocaust and other violence. How does it fit in here? I might have let my parents' fear make me afraid. They are fearful people, not surprisingly, and have never understood my life choices. I've felt I've been working against something my whole adult life, and now that I am where I want to be, happily alone, listening to this made me wonder if I'd been working against this idea of being "loaded for vulnerability", against some inheritance, refusing to give in to it. Refusing to depend on anyone else, for my survival, for my happiness. Yes, that's it. That's it.

I have thought it through, she says.

Go on, I say.

My brother was here, she says. Last week. And we haven't... we don't... I mean, spend much time together. Not for years. So we went out for dinner, and I know he used to want to be in a relationship, to have children. I asked if he still did. If he was, you know, dating. It felt weird to be asking, but also it's part of life, right? He said he did want that, and yes, he was going on dates, but he didn't go into details, and that's fine. And then he asked me. He said I had said once that I'd "given up all that", and I was trying to explain the other night what that meant. It was really only afterwards – and after I was re-telling this to a friend the other day – that I've come up with what I should have said. I think he thought my "giving up" was giving up on finding the right person to be with. But that would still be me subscribing to the Right Person story. And what I've given up, or let go of, or stepped out of, is the story itself. It's like you wouldn't keep looking for the perfect cheese, say, if you decided you didn't believe in dairy products as a foodstuff. If you were a vegan, although that's more abstinence than stepping out of the story. Or is it that? I'm not sure. But anyway, I haven't given up, I've stepped out of.

Alright, I say. I think I understand your meaning. But someone who is still inside that story may not understand, is that what you're saying? They may not be able to hear it.

Yes, I think it is, she says. I was trying to tell my Dad, too, a few days later, but he really doesn't understand, can't imagine me being happy "on my own". "On my own" is a judgement, isn't it? Like the word "single", which implies "less than". I own me. I am not owned by anyone else. Or it does inside that particular story. So, it's Christmas Eve now, and I'm home alone and this is exactly where I want to be and how I want to be. I watched a film, by a writer-director who is known for her films about women. But this one was about a middle-aged man who has left his wife in search of happiness. And it was very well made, it pressed all the right buttons, so as the end credits rolled I thought it was a good film. But a few minutes later, I realised it wasn't. In terms of story, nothing had changed, he hadn't changed, shifted. The final scene was him cooking dinner for his new girlfriend, and I thought: Is it implying he's found happiness? Or is the look he gave at the end hinting that he knows he hasn't, that he's just repeating what he did before?

He tried to step out of the story but hasn't really stepped out? I say.

Exactly! He tried really hard, he did all sorts of things that his ex and his former friends didn't understand – taking drugs, spending time talking to teenagers, trying to find what he had felt he'd lost. But he couldn't resist the pull of that story. And I wondered what it is about aloneness, about solitude, that frightens people, that makes them – us, humans – even need this story in the first place. The friend I was telling about the conversation with my brother, she understands, she's stepped out of the story too, although in a different way to me. And another female friend posted online about being blissfully alone for Christmas. So I thought my way through it. I thought first: scared of being alone? Is that: scared of being with yourself? And I thought – but we are never "without" ourselves, so can we be "with" ourselves?

This is sounding as if you were having a philosophical debate, I say.

I was! she says. I haven't done this for a while, it was such fun, following the trail of my thoughts. So, if not scared of being "with" yourself, then scared of being yourself. I looked around my living room, which I have set up exactly to please me, it is how I want it, and I don't have to please anyone, and I thought about how I am unfettered, unseen. And how another person, even the most wonderful, giving, thoughtful Other, sees and fetters you. There must be a way we can't be when another person is around, even when I'm with that one person I love being with as much as I love being alone. It's a few percent less, or different; I am seen, I am ever-so-slightly fettered. But here, now, in the room designed just for me, I wondered who wouldn't want this. Why wouldn't someone want this? Because they don't want to be themselves. Like Hannah, perhaps, in that article, the one about the fugue states? Why wouldn't someone want to be themselves? Because they are worried about what might arise when they are alone.

The phrase "dark urges" came into my mind, she says, and I wondered what I meant by that. I haven't had any dark urges, being alone doesn't do that for me. I sometimes get sad, or angry at something, but not in a way that's different from when I wasn't living alone. There are no specially dark urges or awful thoughts. And I thought: Is this the essence of it, the fear that by being alone you will discover that you are not a good person? That there is something rotten in you?

People avoid solitude, they ask to be fettered so that they will never find out. But they forget – or choose not to imagine, or aren't able to imagine – the other option: that they might find out that not only are they not a bad person, they are rather wonderful. They think they're avoiding looking into the darkness – like the guy in the film who sat there watching old home movies and focussing on what he doesn't have anymore, the cliché of divorce, of loneliness. What if actually they might be avoiding looking into the light, not into darkness? Because that's how it feels to me, the aloneness lets in the light. I see it. There are others who know this, too. The Buddhists, say, with their silent retreats.

Yes, I say. Go on.

And that reminded me, she says, of the mindfulness retreat I went on a few years ago. It was a beginners course and when the organisers suggested we try a six-hour silence, quite a few people panicked. For me, the idea was heavenly. I didn't understand their panic. But now I see what they might have been scared of: that left alone with their thoughts, untethered, unrestrained, they would discover how awful they were.

Did they? I say.

Nope, she says. Everyone was totally blissed out by it!

So it is a fear that has very little basis in reality, I say.

Yes, she says slowly. I can't understand where it's come from, why people would be so scared of themselves, of some thing they think might be in there, as if they don't know themselves at all. And they don't want to. Why would our default be to think we were bad people? Is it something evolution has done to make us to couple up and procreate? There's that idea of original sin in Christianity, does it come from that? But you'd think that seeing yourself as wonderful, that loving yourself, would make you want to make more copies of yourself and that could lead to procreation too, a much happier procreation!

I do like the way your thoughts are going, I say. Towards happiness.

Towards happiness! she says. All of it could be, couldn't it? Am I missing something in my argument, some logical step?

I don't see anything, I say.

I mean, what other reason can there be for this fear of being alone? Too scared to be too happy on your own? Another cliché: You'll get "set in your ways". Is that to frighten us not to be too happy, because the entire industry based around the story of romantic pairings might wobble? Why wouldn't I want to be set in my ways if my ways are joyous, if my ways make me feel right, make feel like I am a rather wonderful person to be around?

Quite, I say.

There is a swan on its own on the lake, which is "unusual", says a woman passing by, and we speculate, since there is the assumption of swans mating for life, what has happened to its partner. "Dead, perhaps," she says, but later, when I'm on my own, projecting wildly of course, I think: Well, maybe this swan likes solitude, doing whatever it wants. (I resisted thinking "she"; I didn't project on her completely.)

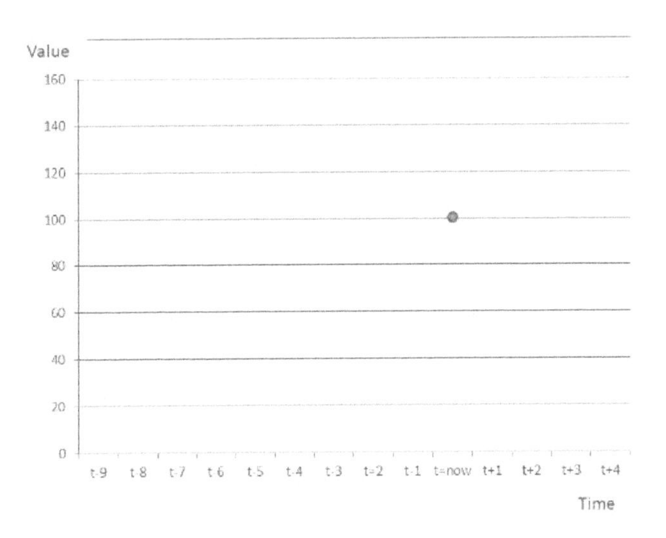

The swan = a single data point. We are used to things coming in pairs, in sets, in groups. What do we do with a solitary? Once there is a second, a line can be drawn between them, there is a relationship, we can say something. And a group, oh my, so much data, look at everything we might infer! We might try for a pattern here, the similarities, the differences. We might theorise cause and effect. Give us at least two: one point is floating; one point says nothing.

What if I want to float. What if I don't want to give you any information, don't want to be related, labelled, part of your pattern.

Take your instruments and leave.

The dead are very interested in this idea of swans, of the unusualness of the single swan. Some of them, men of science – yes, so few women of science, too few – nod their heads at the single point, the need for data, for a relation between things.

Some of the women, thinking of that swan, thinking of the woman and her singleness, want to tell her, Yes, refuse! No labels, they want to say to her. Be that swan, be moving, be on your own lake. There is a rustling across the cemetery, down and along, a whispering about cause and effect, relationship and solitary. The dead remember one of the woman's poems, one that she read to them so early in her visiting, they think, although they are not timed now and they are not sure what memory is now. The poem was about dancing, about not waiting for someone to ask you, about not having anyone's arm on your shoulder. Dance, whisper the dead. Do not wait.

I have been watching a lot of television and films, she says, and it seems I am primed to zoom in on quotes that speak to what I am writing about. Like Julia Roberts shouting at Javier Bardem at the almost-end of *Eat, Pray, Love*. "Do not tell me what lessons I have and haven't learned in the last year. I do not need to love you to prove that I love myself!" Yes, yes, I know that she ends up with him, but still. I like that she said it at all.

Hollywood, I say, and we laugh.

Yes! she says. They get to something interesting but they can't imagine the audience would want that, would want to see Julia Roberts happily alone. What a scandal, eh! And I've been watching many, many episodes of this medical TV drama, *Grey's Anatomy,* where they are always coupling up, breaking up, getting back together. You know. Drama. One of the characters says to another: "None of this matters if you're alone." She means: You don't want to be Chief of Surgery if you have to give up the person you love. I disagree. Of course. This episode aired 12 years ago. Nothing's changed for us happily-alones. Happily alone does not make for drama. It's not a good story, is it?

You're telling that story and I think it is very good, I say, and then wonder if I have spoken out of turn.

Oh thank you, she says. You might not believe it but that means a lot. I know we have this certain relationship, and you are here to help me in a certain way. But I feel like it's more than that, too, that you want the best for me. Like the ideal friend, the ideal reader, too, maybe.

When she says this this makes me feel. I feel many things, although we are not meant to.

Thank you, I say.

Okay, she says. One more quote, from Meredith, one of the main characters in *Grey's Anatomy:* "It's much better to be alone and feel like a success than to be in a relationship and feel like a failure all the time, right?" I like that. Although of course, the writers didn't let her stay there, in that alone space. Nope.

A shame, I say.

It is, she says. It is.

Go on, I say.

"Because Freud believed that everything was 'overdetermined', had multiple causes and reasons, nothing could be about one thing...From a psychoanalytic point of view what is made of the evidence is always more important (more revealing) than the evidence itself; and what is selected out as evidence, and how it is interpreted – what it is used to do – is a function of unconscious desire."

– Adam Phillips in *Becoming Freud: The Making of a Psychoanalyst*

Why have I selected this quote?

Make of that what you will. I'm not going to explain everything.

I've changed the ending, she says. We haven't spoken for a while, for several months, in fact. She put this away, told me she needed to let it lie, which is always a wise thing to do.

So you read it through? I say.

Yes! she says and she sounds happy.

How was it? I say.

Oh my, she says. I was scared. Ridiculously, stupidly scared of reading it from the beginning all the way to the end, and I don't know what I was scared of. Probably of finding out that it was drivel, a whole year wasted, nothing meaningful, nothing entertaining, nothing to make it into some sort of whole. I am at this writing retreat, in Ireland, and it's beautiful. This is the place I'd set aside for reading it and finishing it. I'd come for this. I warned the others on the first night, that the next day they might find me weeping somewhere. They understood. It's so nice to be around people who get it.

Go on, I say, and I must admit I am somewhat jealous, of these others who get it. But I keep that back. She is finishing. This is what we have worked towards. An ending is our goal. Is it wrong of me to also not want it?

I guess the idea of finishing is also scary, she says, in that way she has of somehow knowing what it is I am thinking. I've never done this before, a whole book, not like this. But you know, she says, and I can hear her voice light up, it was fine! I didn't cry, for either the worst or the best reasons. I was calm. Because I've started another book since then, this isn't my precious baby any more. Letting it lie, standing back. That was the best thing.

What did you think? I say.

What I did panic about, she says, which I'd forgotten, is how autobiographical some of it is! Oh dear. But I decided I wouldn't worry about that yet. I needed to know if something should be in that gap I left, before the ending that I wrote ages ago. So immediately after reading the whole thing, I went for a walk, and as I walked I started to see what I needed to do. And the first thing was to change the ending. It was too neat, too nice. It wasn't the note that I wanted to end on now. Something that came earlier needed to be the final page. Which partly surprised me and partly wasn't a surprise at all.

Neat endings aren't your style, I say.

No! she says. I spend so much time telling people who have sent me their short stories for critique that life isn't like that, all hermetically sealed, happily-ever-after, and it doesn't allow the reader to keep thinking about the story, the characters. But look, I'd done it myself!

You may have needed to do it while you were still writing, knowing it would then be changed, I say.

You are clever, she says, and I admit, this makes me feel better about all those others who get it, because I was the one who got it first. Goodness, this really isn't about me.

What happened next?

The new ending, she says, surprised me because it's who I am now, it's where I am now. And I think that has shifted over the past 18 months. But this is definitely what I want, so I made those changes, and started tweaking, moving some other things around, and taking some stuff out. Nothing is sacred or set in stone, right?

It's your book, I say.

Yes! she says. And this is the final piece. I've waited a few days to tell you. I've been sitting with it, taking it for walks with me, holding the shape of the whole of it and turning it over and around. It's a sort of paradoxical experience, to hold it lightly enough, from a distance, to see it and to feel it. Not to feel how someone else might see it, because I let go of that a long time ago. Just to ask: Is this what I want? Have I said what I needed to say?

And?

I have, she says. I'm pretty sure. Now I send it into the world, first to my agent – and if she agrees – further out. And we see what happens. But does this mean? Is it time?

We have been trained for this moment. I have strict guidelines about it. But it takes me a minute before I am able to speak.

Yes, I say. It is. Yes. Goodbye.

Thank you, she says. Thank you. I couldn't have. I really couldn't have. I will miss you. And I do think maybe you'll... I mean, I don't know if that happens, but will you...?

I don't say anything. I am not supposed to. This is it. It is hard.

Are you still...? she says. Oh gosh. This really is. It really is. Hello?

I hear her sigh. I listening to her breathing for a few minutes.

And then.

And inside the woman was another woman. The outside woman heard the inside woman when she turned down the radio, the television, just before she took her earplugs out in the morning. But the outside woman didn't know what the inside woman was saying. Was she trying to tell her something? The outside woman listened hard, when she could, when it was the right type of quiet.

"Animate?" she murmured. "Sing? Stopcock? Purple?" The outside woman wrote down the inside woman's words, or what she thought she heard, but they didn't make sense to her at all.

You might think the outside woman was the kind to not know herself, the sort to repress her misery, her worries and anxiety. But the outside woman was one of those rare happy types, the ones who come into your room, look at you properly, and who are always smiling. You shouldn't think she was hiding anything. She was right there, when you needed her. I don't know about the inside woman. I can't answer your questions about her.

The outside woman – who lived with a cat, a very contented cat who suited the outside woman perfectly, preferring her own space too – liked to do the crossword, and she wondered if the inside woman was offering her help.

"Medieval," she wrote down alongside the 'across' clue list. "Hydrogen. Premium. Fortitude." But she couldn't make the words fit what she was solving.

One morning the outside woman woke up to rain, a thudding on the roof, no birds at all, and nothing for her to get out of bed for in a hurry. The cat could wait for breakfast. She put her earplugs back in and said to her inside woman:

"Hello?"

Silence. That light buzzing silence through the foam. The outside woman tried again.

"Hello, is there something you…?"

She felt ridiculous. Who was she even talking to? She took out her earplugs, and opened the door to greet the quietly waiting cat.

Five minutes before the outside woman died, many years later, many years after her cat was gone and the cat that came after that, she heard the inside woman clearly for the first time.

"Oh," said the outside woman, who had an idea that death

was at her heels. “I see,” she said, smiling as the inside woman spoke in full sentences at last. “Thank you,” said the outside woman. “Yes, of course, I will,” she whispered to herself as something ended, joined and slipped to light.

The dead say: Don't join us yet.

The dead say: Don't come back. Don't come and walk here anymore.

The dead say: Be angry. Be confused. Be in air. Be in water.

The dead say: Don't forget us. Name us when you can. But don't come and walk here anymore.

We are all together, this is the first time we have met since I finished. Since we said goodbye. Since, as I am meant to think of it, that job came to an end. My Author cracked her shell, she emerged, the birth is over. And I am sitting here, with my colleagues. They are laughing, someone is telling of an Author who ate part of her manuscript and was rushed to hospital.

How did it taste? asks someone.

She didn't mention that! says the Author's Narrator, and we laugh and shake our heads. I laugh and shake my head too.

But I want to ask something. I want to ask this: Who am I now that I don't have an Author? Who am I without that role, with no one to say Go on to? Am I myself?

I miss her, I want to say.

I laugh loudly. I stand up and go over to the bar to buy everyone another round.

When the wolves come, the town is ready. The women stand at the front. They have painted their faces, and the faces of the girls, who are in a row behind them.

The wolves are not a metaphor, the women tell the girls. Their teeth are not symbolic. Their claws are claws. When we say they will eat you, we are not referring to spiritual consumption. They are wolves.

From the forest comes a howling. The women stiffen.

Notes

P17 "Every day, this priest climbs a sheer cliff to get to church", *The Tablet,* 20/2/2018
http://www.thetablet.co.uk/news/8587/every-day-this-priest-climbs-a-sheer-cliff-to-get-to-church

P31 "55 Incredible Photos of Girls Going to School around the World", *Huffington Post,* 8/3/2018
http://www.huffingtonpost.co.uk/entry/55-incredible-photos-of-girls-going-to-school-around-the-world_us_5aa01a8de4b002df2c6014da

P40 "How a Young Woman Lost Her Identity", *New Yorker,* 26/3/2018
https://www.newyorker.com/magazine/2018/04/02/how-a-young-woman-lost-her-identity

P44 "What does she think she looks like", Rosemary Hill, *London Review of Books,* 5/4/2018
https://www.lrb.co.uk/v40/n07/rosemary-hill/what-does-she-think-she-looks-like

P58 "Japan's Rent-a-Family Industry", by Elif Batuman, *New Yorker,* 30/4/2018
https://www.newyorker.com/magazine/2018/04/30/japans-rent-a-family-industry

P108 Oliver Burkeman: *Why Are We So Angry?* BBC Radio 4, 17/10/2018
https://www.bbc.co.uk/programmes/m0000qky

P114 *Inherited Fear,* BBC Radio 4, 18/12/ 2018
https://www.bbc.co.uk/programmes/b09zv3d3

P121 *Eat Pray Love,* film (2010)

P121 Dr Miranda Bailey to Dr Derek Shepherd, *Grey's Anatomy,* Season 3, episode 20, 'Time after Time'

P121 *Grey's Anatomy,* Season 4, episode 1, "A Change is Gonna Come"

Acknowledgements

I would have started writing this book but I highly doubt I would have finished it without the support of my amazing literary agent, Kate Johnson. Her excellent eye and wonderful editing suggestions, as well as her constant faith in of my writing, no matter how odd or "uncommercial", gave me permission to, well, go on. Thank you, Kate, for your friendship and for helping me to tell my story.

Thank you to the staff at Manchester's Southern Cemetery who, when I asked if they had ever had a writer-in-residence, said: "Not a live one". Thank you, Cliff, Ellen, Adam, Peter and Jim, for introducing me to your world, answering my endless questions about what it's like to work in between the living and the dead, for laughing more than any other group of people I've ever met, and for giving me free rein to peer into your record books and wander around the grounds, talking to your inhabitants and looking for women like me.

I had no idea when I began as the Southern Cemetery's writer-in-residence in 2018 that I would end up making a radio documentary about my time there, reading excerpts of this book, and sharing my thoughts on the memorialisation of single people without children in general, and myself in particular. Thank you to the most excellent of producers, Faith Lawrence, who came up with the idea, gently cajoling me into talking as we explored the cemetery by day and at dusk, and who created "Who Will Call Me Beloved?" for BBC Radio 4 and the World Service in 2019 with just as much giggling as I had hoped for. (I'm sorry I was too chicken to stay in the cemetery overnight with you. Next time.)

Thank you to my dear Barmooristas, who listened to and made suggestions about excerpts from this book-in-progress during our semi-annual week-long retreats in deepest Yorkshire. You helped bring this book into being and your support, camaraderie and feeding in all ways mean so much to me.

Thank you to artists Penny Hardy, Shirin Neshat and Amy Sherald for permission to include images of your breathtaking art in this book, it means so much to me that you agreed to their use. The book would not have been the same without them.

And finally, an enormous thank you to my editor and published Aaron Kent for championing risk-taking and experimental writing that doesn't fit into neat boxes and struggles out from under labels. I am so grateful that you took a chance on this strange and uncategorizable book and welcomed me into your Broken Sleep Books family.

Lay out your unrest

Lightning Source UK Ltd.
Milton Keynes UK
UKHW050216191122
412432UK00012B/213

9 781915 079930